"Search." At Marie's one-word command, Astrid tore across the asphalt and disappeared over the edge of the road, her progress marked by swaying tall weeds and grasses.

Marie waited until insistent barking told her Astrid had found something. Pulling out her pepper spray, Marie inched toward the side of the pavement with caution. She peered over the road's shoulder and gasped when she saw what had Astrid so worked up.

A man, covered in filth and blood, lay crosswise in a runoff ditch, his eyes closed.

All hope evaporated the moment she touched him. Despair gripped her insides and twisted. His skin was cold. Deathly cold. And he hadn't moved an inch, not even a slight rise and fall of his chest. With two fingers lightly pressing on the artery in his neck, Marie waited to feel the telltale pulsing of blood. Nothing.

"Come on, mister. Wake up!"

Astrid stopped her pacing, approached the man and licked his face.

In that moment, Marie felt a pulse.

He was alive.

SCENT DETECTION

LESLIE MARSHMAN

HARLEQUIN
INTRIGUE

To the Lunch Bunch.
May our friendship and encouragement last forever!

Special thanks and acknowledgment are given to
Leslie Marshman for her contribution to the K-9s on
Patrol miniseries.

Recycling programs
for this product may
not exist in your area.

ISBN-13: 978-1-335-58205-8

Scent Detection

For questions and comments about the quality of this book,
please contact us at CustomerService@Harlequin.com.

Harlequin Enterprises ULC
22 Adelaide St. West, 41st Floor
Toronto, Ontario M5H 4E3, Canada
www.Harlequin.com

Printed in U.S.A.

Multi-award-winning author **Leslie Marshman** writes novels featuring strong heroines, the heroes who love them and the bad guys who fear them. She called Denver home until she married a Texan without reading the fine print. Now she lives halfway between Houston and Galveston and embraces the humidity. When Leslie's not writing, you might find her camping at a lake, fishing pole in one hand and a book in the other. Visit her at www.lesliemarshman.com, www.Facebook.com/lesliemarshmanauthor, www.Instagram.com/leslie_marshman or @lesliemarshman on Twitter.

Books by Leslie Marshman

Harlequin Intrigue

Resolute Justice
Scent Detection

Visit the Author Profile page at Harlequin.com.

CAST OF CHARACTERS

Marie Beaumont—The only veterinarian in Jasper, Idaho, she also tends to the dogs at Daniels Canine Academy. A private person who keeps to herself as much as possible, she's still considered a newcomer after five years in town.

Jack—A stranger hurt in an accident just outside of Jasper during a violent storm. He claims that due to his head injury, he doesn't know who he is or why he's there, but he refuses to leave town.

Emma Daniels—Owner of Daniels Canine Academy, she trains search and rescue dogs. She and Marie have become friends through working with the dogs.

Jason Wright—An officer with the Jasper Police Department who befriends Jack and helps him find a job and a place to stay.

Dotty Hazzard—A resident of Hemlock Hills Assisted Living Facility, she's become a surrogate grandmother to Marie.

Astrid—Marie's constant companion, the Doberman mix was trained as a guard dog at Daniels Canine Academy.

Chapter One

The truck careened through the night, its driver hell-bent on his objective.

Angry blades of rain slashed across the windshield, cutting visibility to almost nothing. On this lonely stretch of State Highway 95 in Idaho's northwest backcountry, landslides were frequent, streetlights rare. Only wicked forks of lightning, strobing every few seconds off the inky peaks of the Seven Devils Range, revealed the dangerous ledge where the pavement ended and the cliff's steep drop began.

Another blinding flash illuminated a sharp curve up ahead. Exhausted, fueled only by caffeine and adrenaline, the driver's grip tightened on the steering wheel. The truck hydroplaned, spinning across the rain-slick road before stopping on the asphalt's edge. For several long seconds, the vehicle teetered at a precarious angle.

Thunder cracked and shook the ground. The truck's nose dipped farther, held for a moment, then tumbled into the black abyss. Glancing off trees. Plowing over saplings, scrub and rocks. He jammed down on the brakes in a futile attempt to stop the frenzied descent.

Icy fingers of death reached for him, and his gut crawled into his throat as the truck continued its down-hill plunge. His head smashed into the steering wheel before crashing against the side window. Once. Twice. After that he lost the ability to count. To see. To concentrate.

But not to feel pain.

The airbag deployed, ramming into his chest and face like a concrete wall. Air whooshed from his lungs. He fought to take a breath. His face throbbed; blood ran from his nose across his lips. And still, the truck pinballed down the hill, the seat belt digging a sharp groove into his shoulder and torso.

One last hard bump, another crack on the head and the truck came to a jarring halt. Steam hissed from a busted radiator. High-pitched ringing filled the inside of his head, inviting madness. Clouded by pain, he fought the mental chaos until one concept came into focus.

Danger. Must keep moving.

He fumbled to release the restraint cutting across his shoulders, then brushed away shattered windshield glass from his lap, his chest. A warm and sticky wetness streamed from his scalp, over his ear and down his neck. Crushed metal blocked his escape. He found a handle. It wouldn't budge. He rammed his shoulder against the obstruction. Agonizing pain shot up his spine and exploded inside his skull.

Fighting waves of nausea, he continued to throw himself against it until the door gave way with the groan of a dying beast. He tumbled out, landed hard in the mud. Rocks cut his fingers. He groped like a blind man, grabbing small boulders and trees to pull himself up. His hands and feet slipped with each attempt. More ground-shaking thunder. More pain.

Lightning illuminated everything like the ominous sweep of a prison searchlight. Movement drew his gaze uphill. Something black and thick and powerful rolling toward him. Like a gelatinous demon, it consumed branches, rocks, small trees, everything in its path.

Mudslide.

The mix of dirt and rain formed a deadly flow, and he scrambled from its path of destruction. One foot got tangled in the muck and it tried to swallow him. He panicked. Pulled and pulled. With a sucking squelch, a bare foot broke free.

He fell away from the mud. White pain blinded him as he hit his head once more. After clambering to his knees, he crawled sideways from the slide. At a hideous screech of metal, he turned back to look. A flash of lightning spotlighted the flow of mud engulfing his truck and carrying it over a ledge he hadn't known he was sitting on.

The close call paralyzed him.

The barrage of pain muddled his brain.

Keep moving. Hurry.

Clawing his way up the slope, he fought for every inch, lost traction, slid backward, pushed on. Punishing rain stung his face, but the cold eased the throbbing that raged inside his skull. He topped the hill, made it to the pavement. He stumbled like a drunkard down the middle of the road, wind lashing at him with no mercy. A stray tree branch struck him in the back. He fell forward, hands flailing, scraping his face on the pavement.

One breath. Two breaths.

Danger. Keep moving. Danger everywhere. Anywhere.

He lurched up, regained his footing, staggered back to the edge of the road. Fell again, this time sliding downhill. His exhausted body crumpled, landing in a water-filled culvert alongside the road.

One breath. Two breaths. Three.

Get up.

Keep moving.

Danger.

His muscles refused to cooperate. His eyelids refused to stay open. It was all he could do just to keep his head above the water sluicing through the natural ditch.

One breath. Two breaths…

Danger.

The strobing lights behind his eyes dimmed, the ringing in his ears dulled. His last thoughts before losing consciousness were to hurry, to keep moving.

But why?

DESPITE HAVING TO dodge broken branches and patches of mud, remnants from last night's unprecedented storm, Marie Beaumont headed south from town on her normal early morning run. Since settling in Jasper five years ago, she'd honed her list of preferred routes for maximum safety, the only way to guarantee the most enjoyment from her favorite pastime. The metronome-like slap of her shoes on asphalt quieted troubled thoughts and lowered her ever-present anxiety. Even today, watching every step to avoid tripping, it was worth it.

The mountain breezes that flowed into the canyon never smelled fresher than after a summer storm. The temporary reprieve from August's heat lifted Marie's mood, even if the cloudless blue sky foretold the rising temperatures to come.

"More storms coming. Should help with the heat." She glanced down at her running companion, who'd looked up at the sound of Marie's voice. "Right, girl?"

Astrid, her Doberman-beagle mix, bounded alongside in a running version of "heel." Trained at the DCA—Daniels Canine Academy—located on several acres just north of town, the brown-coated beauty rarely left Marie's side. Despite having cause, Marie had vowed not to live her life in fear. However, cowardice and caution were two different things, and Astrid was as much guard dog as loving pet.

Rounding a bend in the road, Astrid froze, sniffing the air, her tail no longer wagging. Marie skidded to a standstill.

Astrid was in her alert, nonaggressive stance, but that could change in an instant if the situation warranted. "What is it, girl?"

Marie's heart rate kicked up a notch as she surveyed the area. Other than butterflies flitting among the wildflowers and a breeze teasing the tall pines, nothing moved. Nothing unusual caught her eye. Still…

Astrid continued to stare at the far side of the road, whining.

"Search." At Marie's one-word command, Astrid tore across the asphalt and disappeared over the edge of the road, her progress marked by tall, swaying weeds and grasses.

Marie waited until insistent barking told her Astrid had found something. Pulling out her pepper spray, Marie inched toward the side of the pavement with caution. She peered over the road's shoulder and gasped when she saw what had Astrid so worked up.

A man, covered in filth and blood, lay crosswise in a runoff ditch, his eyes closed.

As Astrid paced in agitated circles, Marie dropped all pretense of caution and scurried downhill, tossed her phone on the ground and slide into the wet muck beside the man. A large, well-muscled man, maybe early thirties, whose skin bore a whitish-blue tint that caused Marie's stomach to churn. She reached for his neck, praying to find a pulse.

All hope evaporated the moment she touched him. Despair gripped her insides and twisted. His skin was cold. Deathly cold. And he hadn't moved an inch, not even a slight rise and fall of his chest. With two fingers lightly pressing on the artery in his neck, Marie waited to feel the tell-tale pulsing of blood. Nothing.

"Come on, mister. Wake up!"

Astrid stopped her pacing, approached the man and licked his face.

In that moment, Marie felt a pulse.

He was alive.

She'd already had far too much contact with death, and Marie took a deep breath, grateful that today would not lay more at her feet. Then, she swung into motion.

Astrid wasn't the only one with training, and Marie wasted no more time. As Jasper's one and only veterinarian, she worked with both large and small animals and was no stranger to moving heavy, unresponsive patients. Something had dammed up the ditch farther down from their position, and the pooling water crept toward the man's face.

Running muddy hands over his body, she checked him for broken bones. His head and neck were aligned, a good sign. Ribs okay. Arms and legs, check, check.

The water continued rising, lapping at his chin. Injured or not, she had to move him. She got behind him and shoved him to a seated position. Feeling along his spine, she found no obvious breaks or injuries.

Kneeling on the edge of the ditch, she hooked her elbows beneath his armpits and pulled with all her strength. He barely moved. She slid down behind him, braced her feet and wrapped her arms around his chest. She tugged. Her feet sank in the muck. She braced again, pulled again. She couldn't get traction in the wet, muddy ground. He slid down even lower than before.

The water kept rising. His mouth would soon be covered. Then his nose. Overwhelmed by a strong certainty that she was meant to save this man, Marie called for Astrid. Pulling the shoulder of the man's shirt up, away from his skin, she let Astrid grab it with her teeth.

"Pull, girl!" There would be no drowning on her watch.

She again looped her arms under his shoulders, and together she and Astrid hauled until his chest cleared the water. Grabbing his belt with both hands, Marie planted her feet and dragged his torso out of the culvert. Astrid took over belt duty to keep him from tumbling back into the water as Marie worked one of his legs up and over the edge.

She issued the pull command again. Gripping the belt tighter in her mouth, Astrid yanked. Marie hopped back down and put her shoulder into shoving the rest of the man up and over the lip of the ditch.

"Good job, Astrid."

Marie climbed out of the culvert, sweaty, muddy, trying to catch her breath. Moving with speed, she rolled the man onto his back, confirmed his breathing passage remained clear, then checked his pulse again. Weak, but there. Unconscious, but still alive.

With hands shaking from exertion and the subsiding rush of adrenaline, Marie reached for her cell phone. Only 5 percent juice, but enough. With the power out during the storm, she should have remembered to check it before she left this morning. She dialed 911.

Astrid sniffed the stranger from head to foot, then sat back on her haunches.

Relieved help was now on the way, Marie sank to the ground next to the man and inspected his head wound. "Well, mister, it's not deep, but it's still going to need stitches."

Astrid cocked her head to one side, as if questioning Marie's professional opinion.

"Oh, hush. Just because I'm a vet and not a people doctor doesn't mean I don't know about cuts."

Astrid woofed in reply.

"Really? You think you know better? Listen here, a cut's a cut, no matter how many legs the patient has."

A contrite Astrid came up to her, placed one paw on Marie's arm and slobbered a kiss on her chin.

"Yes, baby. I know. I love you, too." Marie scratched behind the dog's ears.

Astrid settled down, and Marie's attention returned to the man. Her gaze moved from his ripped polo shirt to his mud-soaked jeans, then down to his feet, one wearing only a sock, the other completely bare. "How the heck did you wind up in this situation?"

She looked around but didn't spot a vehicle. She frowned at Astrid. "A hiker?" Astrid tilted her head. "Okay, you're right. Not dressed for it. A tourist maybe?"

Astrid had no response to that question, and no wonder. Marie steered clear of strangers. Other than the few people in Jasper she did know, most thought her standoffish. Someone with trust issues, she'd heard whispered, which she supposed was true, although that wasn't why she avoided strangers. Not by a long shot.

She gave a mental shrug. Whatever people thought about her, she was not the kind of woman who could let this guy, or anyone for that matter, drown in a ditch.

Smoothing back his dirty brown hair, she studied his face, as if by looking at him she could tell what kind of character he had. "Once the blood and mud are washed off, I have a feeling you'll clean up good."

She twisted her lips, amused at her train of thought. "Not that I care about that, mind you. What I really care about is, are you a good person?" She continued to caress his forehead with the same gentleness she used on injured and abandoned animals.

It didn't surprise her that what drew her most to this man was the helplessness of his situation. Imagine being discovered alone, unconscious and nearly drowned in a water-filled ditch smack-dab in the middle of Nowhere, Idaho. Whatever had befallen him, his plight reeked of the loneliness Marie lived with every day.

His eyelids fluttered open, and just that fast Marie's empathy vanished as her instinctual wariness reared up. Gray eyes met hers with an eerie intensity that seemed to reach for her darkest secrets. That gaze, somehow so knowing, punched an icy blast of foreboding through Marie's chest and froze the breath in her lungs.

A second later, Astrid jumped up as the distant wail of an ambulance siren grew louder. The man's eyes drifted closed, and Marie breathed a sigh of relief. What a strange, unnerving moment that had been.

"Stay," she told Astrid before dashing up the incline to wave down the EMTs.

The ambulance stopped and two paramedics jumped out, one smiling when he saw her. "Hey, Doc. Didn't know you were the one who called this in. What can you tell me about our John Doe?"

Marie knew Eddie, which calmed her jangled nerves even more. She relayed to both paramedics what she knew, which wasn't much, and within minutes the patient was triaged, stabilized and loaded in the ambulance.

"You riding in with us?" Eddie asked her, eyeing her soaking-wet, mud-splattered jogging gear.

Marie looked down. "Oh, wow. I'm quite a mess, aren't I?"

"The uniform of heroes if you ask me. Besides, we have towels for just such emergencies."

Marie patted Astrid's head. "Can my muddy companion come, too?"

Eddie's smile broadened. "You think I'd leave Killer's sweetheart behind? Muddy or not?" He opened both passenger doors of the ambulance's four-door cab. "Even have a harness she can use."

Eddie's Chihuahua, Killer, was a patient of Marie's, and the pint-sized pooch had developed a mastiff-sized crush on Astrid. Marie and Eddie always shared a good laugh whenever the two dogs were together, joking that Killer would need a ladder to take the relationship any further.

Marie got Astrid buckled into the backseat, then climbed in to ride shotgun. Definitely one of the perks of small-town living.

Lights flashing, siren screaming, they sped up the road to Jasper Memorial. During the short ride, Eddie, bless him, rambled on about this and that, oblivious to Marie's noncommittal murmurs and nods. Her focus was squarely centered on the man in the back, no doubt getting hooked up to an IV and being covered in a heat-generating blanket.

She had no reason to fear the stranger. Anyone could have found him. It was just coincidence that she and Astrid happened to. But coincidence was simply not something that existed in Marie's world, and she couldn't stop herself from imagining the countless ways her Good Samaritan act today might come back to haunt her.

Borrowing trouble, her grandmother had called it.

As much as she hated what it might mean to her well-ordered life, it was time to call George Murphy.

THE HOSPITAL ADMISSIONS nurse tapped a tuneless beat with her pen against the desk. "You must have *some* relationship with the patient. You rode in the ambulance with him."

Marie summoned her patience. "I promise you, I *don't* have a relationship with him. I found him on the side of the road and called 911. I'm happy to give you my contact information, but I don't know the man from Adam." She handed the nurse her driver's license. "As long as you're adding me as a contact, would it be possible to keep me informed of his status?"

Until she spoke to George, the most important thing would be keeping an eye on the mystery man. Her safety might depend on it, after all. And as a caring person, of course Marie was concerned about his medical status. She always followed up on her patients. Even the tall, handsome one with gray eyes whose life she saved.

The admissions nurse lifted her gaze from her computer screen and gave Marie a somewhat disapproving look, then handed her license back. "Unless the patient gives us permission, we can't release his medical information. But no doubt the police will want you to stick around. They'll need a statement, I would imagine. Maybe they could check with his doctor for you."

"Thank you."

Marie found a chair in the corner of the waiting room where Astrid would be less noticeable. When they had trailed through the ER door behind Eddie, the nurse began scolding her for bringing a dog into the hospital. Eddie had simply said, "Service dog," on his way past the desk and that seemed to mollify her. While it was true that Astrid was a sort of service dog, Marie felt more comfortable keeping a low profile.

Her phone battery was down to 2 percent. Before it went dead, she checked her messages. None. Pretty typical unless there was an animal emergency. Then she dashed off a quick text to Liz, Marie's office manager, letting her know she'd be late getting in to the office, deciding last-minute that the why-she-was-going-to-be-late explanation was too much for a text. She'd just pushed Send when Officer Jason Wright of the Jasper PD strolled up to her.

With cropped black hair, dark brown eyes and a charming smile, the six-foot, muscular rookie officer was engaged to Tashya, the vet tech employed at the Daniels Canine Academy. Which meant Marie saw him often and knew him better than most of the local cops.

"Hi, Jason. I was hoping they'd send you."

He favored her with a sly grin. "Why? 'Cause you like my biceps?" He curled his arm and gave her a flex.

Marie couldn't help it. She grinned back. Extending her arms, placing her wrists together as if in handcuffs, she said, "You busted me. Just promise you won't tell Tashya." For the first time since finding John Doe, Marie felt a measure of calm. Jason had that way about him, a way of brightening a room and easing tension just by being in it.

"I make no promises. Tashya can always tell when I'm lying, so I find it best not to do it."

Wouldn't that be nice. A stab of jealousy pierced Marie. What would it be like to live in a world not consumed by lies?

Jason pulled a small notebook and pen from his pocket. "So, you found our John Doe, huh?"

Nodding, she filled him in on the particulars. He asked a few additional questions, which she answered while he jotted down notes, then he snapped the notebook closed and pocketed it. "That's one lucky dude, if you ask me. Hey, listen, if I have any follow-up questions, I'll just call you, okay?"

"Sure thing."

"You heading home? Need a lift?"

"Thanks, but I think I'll wait here a bit longer. I want to make sure he's okay."

"You might want to rethink that," Jason said with a knowing wink, giving her an up-and-down once-over. "You look a bit like the Creature from the Black Lagoon."

Marie chortled when she glanced down at herself. "What? Is soggy and mud splattered not my best look?"

"Well…"

"Don't answer that. Wouldn't want you lying."

"Whew!" He laughed with her, and then said, "Look, I'm not planning to stick around much longer, but if he wakes up before I leave, I'll let you know."

"Thanks, Jason." She watched him walk away. When he and Tashya tied the knot in a couple of weeks, they would be one of the lucky couples who makes it. Love like theirs gave others in town hope for their own eventual happily-ever-after.

She scoffed.

Not you, Marie. Get a grip.

She probably should leave, grab a shower, forget all about John Doe.

But she wouldn't. Not yet, anyway. She couldn't ignore that look he'd given her, and how it had stirred something within her. Curiosity, certainly. Caution, that was a given. Maybe even a touch of fear. But there was more, something akin to desire, and that was absolutely a path she couldn't afford to go down.

So instead, she worked to convince herself this was just her normal MO. Since early childhood, she'd felt a calling to take in wounded animals and nurse them back to health. And that's what this man reminded her of. A wounded stray who needed her. Well, maybe not her, but someone.

"Dr. Beaumont?"

Startled, Marie looked up at a nurse in scrubs. "Yes?"

"The patient is waking up. Officer Wright and Dr. Saul wondered if you'd join them in the ER."

"Okay if Astrid comes with me?" She grabbed hold of the harness.

"Absolutely. Dr. Saul happens to be a big believer in the power of four-legged companionship." Yet another perk of small-town life.

With Astrid at her side, Marie followed the nurse through the hands-free doors of the ER.

The man at the center of her consternation lay propped against several pillows, his bed partially elevated. He was hooked to an IV bag, a bandage covered the side of his head and most of the mud had been cleaned from his face.

Marie almost sighed in delight. John Doe most definitely cleaned up good. Maybe too good. She stepped closer to his hospital bed, taking in his five-o'clock stubble that gave him an outdoorsy look. Wispy, abstract streaks of white filled the irises of his gray eyes, pulling her in like a black hole in space. She took a deep breath, then exhaled to try to slow her pulse.

His brows pinched into a frown above an unsmiling mouth. Hardly the reaction she expected. Could be as simple as him noticing her less-than-tidy appearance. Or perhaps he was sizing her up, as she had done him. *Hmm.* Just so long as his penetrating stare didn't hide anything more sinister.

Dr. Saul looked up from his clipboard. "Ah, here she is." Wearing a white coat over green scrubs and with a stethoscope dangling around his neck, he was average height, bald and bespectacled. Possibly in his sixties, but Marie never had been good at guessing ages.

The doctor tucked his clipboard to his chest and

spoke to the patient. "Do you mind me discussing your medical condition in front of this woman? I was hoping she might help fill in the blanks, as it were, since she was the one who fished you out of a water-filled ditch this morning. According to Officer Wright here, you would have drowned if not for her."

The man, whose name she still didn't know, said nothing. Only gazed at her with the same disturbing intensity as he had on the side of the road. Finally, Marie grew warm with discomfort.

"Glad to see you're awake. And I don't deserve all the credit. I had a little help this morning." She looked down at Astrid and gave her a pat.

"Sorry, I don't remember." His eyes lingered on her face. "Apparently, I don't even remember *me*."

Dr. Saul rested a sympathetic hand on the man's shoulder. "Our patient is suffering from retrograde amnesia, or the loss of existing and previously made memories. This type of amnesia tends to affect recently formed memories first. Then, if the condition persists, it affects older memories, such as those from childhood. I'm working on transferring him to St. Luke's Hospital in Boise to see a neurologist there who specializes in this sort of thing."

The man with no name continued to stare at Marie, as if paying no attention to the doctor's words. You'd think someone facing such a diagnosis would be more interested in what the doctor was saying than in puzzling out her role in things.

"Seems he can't remember anything before waking up in the ER," Dr. Saul went on. "Not his identity, not how he came to be out in the storm, not even how he received his wounds. And as he said, he doesn't remember being rescued, either."

"He didn't have any ID in his pockets, but he was wearing this." Jason held up a man's watch. "The back is engraved with the name Jack."

"Then I guess we'll call you Jack." Marie smiled and held out her hand toward him. "I'm Marie."

He returned her smile, but it seemed like an automatic response rather than anything genuine. "Nice to meet you, Marie." Jack clasped her hand and held on to it longer than necessary. His touch, warm and strong, sent a pang of loss through her. It had been a long time since she'd experienced a man's touch. Then she raised her chin and shoved the foolish sentiment away. She'd made her own decisions. No point wishing for what she couldn't have.

"Thank you for saving my life." His smile faded, replaced by another disconcerting frown.

Tipping his bandaged head to one side, he studied her face as if trying to piece together a puzzle. But his next words left Marie reeling.

"Didn't you used to be a blonde?"

Chapter Two

Jack's question played on an endless loop in Marie's head as she and Astrid jogged home from the hospital.

Didn't you used to be a blonde?

Her blondes-have-more-fun days ended five years ago when she entered witness protection, WITSEC, after testifying against domestic terrorist Abel Gaines. Marie wasn't even her real name. Neither was Beaumont. As soon as she'd stepped off the witness stand, she left behind everything—and everyone—she loved. She'd chopped off her waist-length ash-blond locks, read the directions on a box of Rich Chestnut hair color and gone into hiding. In Jasper, Idaho.

The instant Marie got home and locked her front door, she reached for the charging cord and plugged in her dead phone. Seconds later she dialed Deputy US Marshal George Murphy, her witness protection case deputy. It went straight to voice mail. *Great.*

"George, this is Marie Beaumont. Call me. SOS. I repeat, SOS."

By the time she ended the call, the phone had recharged enough to show a missed call from Emma,

owner of Daniels Canine Academy. In her voice message, Emma left an urgent plea. A pregnant stray had
wandered in from the storm last night with a broken
leg and needed her attention ASAP.

What was it about this storm and wounded strays?

Marie took a quick shower, decided not to bother
with makeup and tied her *brown* hair—thank you very
much, Mr. I Can't Remember Anything Except You
Used to Be a Blonde—back into a damp ponytail. She
and Astrid made it to the academy in record time.

Before turning off her ignition, she tried her case
deputy again. It went to voice mail again. For a man
supposedly available twenty-four/seven, his absence
troubled her.

Marie's fingers curled around the steering wheel as
the past, which she fought so hard to forget, drew her
back to what a sweet-talker Abel Gains had been. In
the beginning, anyway. How carefully he'd shielded
her from his twisted side until it was almost too late.

Oh, there'd been clues, if she hadn't been too smit-
ten to notice. But then, she'd always sucked at picking
men. Still, even for her, falling for a delusional domestic terrorist in charge of a band of more delusional
domestic terrorists had been the cherry on top of her
disastrous dating life.

A rap on her window startled her. Emma Daniels
peered through the dark tint, her brows pulled together
in concern. "You okay?"

Nodding, Marie turned off the engine, unbuckled
her seat belt, then Astrid's. Trained as a guard dog at

the academy, Astrid fidgeted with pent-up eagerness, but stayed.

"Patience, girl." Marie pushed the door open. The well-trained Doberman struggled to contain her excitement and only leaped from the car when Marie gave the command. Sitting at Emma's feet, Astrid looked up at her, waiting…waiting…

Emma finally took pity on her. "Come here, my sweet girl." Although strong, Emma staggered under fifty pounds of enthusiastic dog greeting. "Good girl, Astrid. I'm happy to see you, too." She commanded Astrid to sit, then turned to Marie. "Okay, it was kind of weird seeing you sitting here in your car, looking all serious. Are you sure you're all right?"

Emma's concern plucked at Marie's loneliness chord, and the truth longed to come out. Marie hated lying, especially to the people she considered friends. But she'd told the truth, the whole truth, nothing but the truth once before. About Abel and his compound full of fanatics, and now her life was one endless lie. WITSEC had its rules, and to stay alive, Marie followed them. No matter how much she hated it.

She pasted a smile on her face. "Just a little rattled, is all. During our run this morning, Astrid found a man unconscious on the side of the road." She reached into the back of her RAV4 and grabbed her vet bag. "I called 911, then rode with him to the hospital." Marie shrugged. "I wanted to make sure he was okay, you know?"

Emma's eyes rounded in sympathy as she reached for Marie and gave her a warm hug. "Of course, you did. You never pass up a chance to help an injured creature." Standing back, Emma gave her a knowing smile. "Does he happen to be young and good-looking? Single, perhaps? I happen to know a vet who is young, good-looking and single."

Marie's cheeks warmed. "You know I'm not looking for a man."

Emma huffed. "I don't see why not. And you've never bothered to explain it to me, either. Your reticence is one of the most annoying things about you if you ask me."

With one eyebrow cocked, Marie held Emma's gaze for a beat before speaking. "And I didn't."

"Okay, okay." Emma raised both hands in surrender. "I'll back off. For now. How's he doing, anyway, your two-legged stray?"

Astrid heeled along Marie's left side as they all walked toward the kennel, knowing if she behaved now, she would be let loose once they got inside.

"No broken bones, but a serious concussion. And amnesia, apparently."

"Amnesia?" Emma whistled, which had Astrid's ears twitching. "I didn't think that was really a thing. Just a plot device they use in books and movies."

"Oh, no. It's real enough. Just not very common."

Emma opened the door to the kennel and Astrid looked up at her with round, pleading eyes. "Free." Hearing her release word, Astrid ran off to sniff around and get reacquainted with the other academy residents.

Marie followed Emma toward the last stall on the left. Although the building could handle twelve dogs at one time, with six inside stalls and connected outdoor runs on each side of the building, it wasn't at full capacity right now.

Emma unlatched the stall door. "Here's our little mama-to-be. I found her out behind the barn when I checked on the horses last night." A small, emaciated black Lab cowered in the corner of the space, shivering despite the warm day.

"Aggressive?" Marie asked.

"Nope. Not so far. Just the opposite, in fact."

Marie noticed the bowls of food and water. "Has she eaten anything?"

"Not a bite, but she did take a bit of water. She hasn't had anything since midnight, though."

Marie crouched and held her hand out, palm up. The dog stared at her with plaintive eyes. "You must have been terrified in that storm. Where'd you come from, I wonder?"

Emma's words turned hard, though her tone remained calm. "Well, wherever it was, based on her injuries, I don't want her going back. Between the broken leg and abrasions on her sides, my guess is someone tossed her out of a moving vehicle. Either that or she was unrestrained in the bed of a truck and flew out."

The dog quivered with fear, so Marie let her sniff her hand for a few minutes before she started the exam. Her front right leg was bent at an odd angle due to the fractured bone. Bloody patches of matted hair and raw scrapes that looked like road rash covered her. Aside from the fresh wounds, old scars from previous injuries told a story of abuse.

"Poor girl. You've had it rough, haven't you? Not to

worry. I've got you now. You and your babies are going to be just fine." Marie glanced up at Emma. "I'm going to sedate her so I can move her to my office and properly set the leg. While she's out, I'll check her for internal injuries and clean up her other wounds. I might have to take the puppies instead of waiting for natural labor. Hopefully, I won't have to."

Turning her attention back to the dog, Marie stroked the soft fur on her head, one of the few places not bloodied. A wave of déjà vu swept over her. Just a few hours earlier, she'd smoothed hair back from the man's—no, *Jack's*—face. Were the two somehow connected beyond the circumstances of the storm? Or had fate simply placed the same healer in the path of two injured parties in one morning?

"Well, you know how I feel about animal abuse." Emma picked up the dog's dishes to keep Astrid from having a midday snack. "So, you just add the surgery and whatever care she needs to my tab."

"Don't be silly. This one's on the house." True, Marie's tight budget meant she could ill afford the cost, but she often treated strays pro bono.

"Hmph. Unless someone can prove they're the owner and that they weren't responsible for this girl's injuries, I'll soon have a whole litter of future search and rescue dogs that you'll need to be tending. So, I *insist* on paying."

Marie, still focused on the Lab, couldn't help but smile at just how stubborn Emma probably looked right now. She may not be able to tell Emma the entire truth of her life, but she thanked her lucky stars to have her as a friend. "How 'bout this? I'll take care of the surgery, then bring her back here and Tashya can handle her aftercare." Marie finally looked over her shoulder at Emma. As expected, Emma's hands were on her hips.

"All right, all right." She dropped her hands to her sides. "Thank you. I don't know how we got along before you moved to town."

"Can you come keep her calm?"

Emma did just that while Marie took a syringe from her medical bag and injected the dog, who was soon asleep. "Let's give her a few more minutes before we move her."

After some well-earned free time, Astrid followed her nose back to Marie. Coming alongside her owner, Astrid approached the injured dog one sniff at a time. She stopped about a foot away, lay down on the floor and whined in sympathy.

"You got it, Doc." Emma stood and leaned against the wall. "So, about your two-legged rescue, any more to the story?"

Marie refused to break one of her cardinal rules. But if she couldn't tell Emma the whole truth, she could at least allude to the possible danger the man presented. "There's something odd about his situation. I mean, beyond the whole amnesia thing. The guy said he had no idea where he was from. When Jason asked him where he thought he might have been heading, he wasn't sure about that either. But here's the strange part. Right after that, he said somehow 'this place' felt right."

"This place? As in the hospital?" Emma's nose wrinkled in puzzlement.

Marie gestured with her arm in a large arc. "No. *This* place, as in Jasper. He seems to think Jasper is where he belongs. But Jason told me in confidence there aren't any missing person reports on anyone fitting his description."

Emma frowned. "Okay, that's a little weird."

Then she tilted her head, reminding Marie of Astrid.

"But try thinking about it from his point of view," Emma continued. "It's got to be strange. To know things, but not understand the context."

Marie conceded her friend's point with a small nod.

Emma crossed to a stack of freshly laundered dog towels and folded the top one. "He doesn't remember anything about his past?"

Marie shook her head. "Nope. Nothing. The only thing he had with him was a watch engraved with a name on the back."

"Wait. He has a name?"

"Yeah. Well, maybe. Jack."

"Hmmm, Jack," Emma said, trying it on for size as she folded more towels. "Nice enough. What's going to happen to him?"

"His doctor's going to transfer him to St. Luke's in Boise, to see some neurologist who deals with memory loss and claims of amnesia." Marie repacked her vet bag. "Said it's the best option for him."

And for me.

After being convicted, Abel had sworn she'd never be safe again. And he was the type of man who made good on his promises. That threat had taken her into witness protection and given her reason to avoid strangers.

Given that Jasper was a year-round tourist town, from skiing in the winter to fishing and white water rafting in the summer, avoiding strangers was a full-time occupation. No matter how hard she tried to live a quiet life, she couldn't help but wonder if every unknown set of eyes that lingered on her just a bit too long might be one of Abel's men. Made sense that getting Jack out of town, and off her mind, gave her one less stranger to worry about.

Emma cocked a brow. "What do you mean, 'claims of amnesia?' You think this guy is faking it?" She left the stall, returning a minute later with a pet carrier.

"Could be." Marie's shrug felt a bit defensive. "Like I said, amnesia is pretty rare." She hefted her bag from one hand to the other. "I mean, think about it. How would anyone know if he was telling the truth?"

Emma chuckled. "You really are the most untrusting person I know."

"And you're entirely too trusting," Marie countered, even knowing her friend was right. She lined the carrier with some of Emma's clean towels, then lifted the stray in. "Can you bring my bag? I'll carry the dog."

Astrid whined and Emma scratched behind her ear. "Aren't you getting enough attention, girl?"

"Oh, she never gets *any* attention. I completely ignore her all day." Marie crouched down and rubbed Astrid's chest. "You poor neglected thing, you."

She stood and lifted the carrier with both hands, waiting for Emma to open the door for her. Astrid dashed out and was waiting next to the RAV4 by the time the women arrived.

Marie loaded the carrier into her car. "I'll call you tonight and let you know how our girl is doing. And in a few days, when she's recovered enough to move her, I'll bring her back."

"When you do, would you mind looking at Elton's foot for me? I thought I saw him favoring it this morning, but I might be wrong."

Elton, a black-and-white Appaloosa, was one of Emma's two rescue horses. The other one, a brown American quarter horse, she'd named Presley. Marie wondered which singer was up next if Emma rescued a third horse.

"Sure. Want me to do it now?"

Emma shook her head. "The dog's injuries are much worse and way more time-sensitive. I'll keep an eye on Elton."

Marie stuck her hand out the window and waved as she drove away. On the way back to town, she focused once more on her two-legged stray. She recalled how Granny Mae used to tell her curiosity killed the cat and that if Marie wasn't careful, it would get her, too.

And so it had. Sticking her nose into someone else's business was exactly how her life had taken a dangerous, unexpected detour. To Jasper, Idaho. A place where the stranger insisted he belonged.

Didn't you used to be a blonde?

Marie Beaumont.

Cooped up in a hospital room for three long, frustrating, boring days, Jack—at least he thought he was Jack—could conjure little else in his otherwise blank head. Why, when he could remember nothing else, did she seem familiar to him? Especially puzzling given that she couldn't say the same about him.

His natural inclination—and yes, he'd apparently retained inclinations—was to distrust her. Amnesia be damned. She was hiding something. He knew that for certain. Down deep in his gut, where instinct was ingrained and not dependent on memory, he knew. Wouldn't that mean she knew him, too?

The patrolman, Jason, confirmed she'd been the town's vet since moving to Jasper five years ago. If they had known each other, it was in a past Jack couldn't remember. According to the friendly cop, Dr. Marie Beaumont was a bit of a loner, and no one knew much about her life before she'd shown up in itty-bitty Jasper, Idaho, out of the blue and with no relatives to draw her here. Well, regardless of the reason that brought her here, Jack owed her his life.

And speaking of Jasper, why Jack felt a connection to the place when clearly no one here knew him was anyone's guess. Maybe it wasn't a person, but the place itself that called to him. He'd borrowed Jason's phone and scrolled through pictures of the town, but nothing triggered his dormant memories. Talk about maddening.

Then there was Jason, himself. The young officer made it a point to visit him each day. Like a friend. Only they weren't. Not that Jack was about to look a gift horse in the mouth. His physical injuries were healing, but conversations that didn't involve his medical chart were a breath of fresh air.

A rap sounded on the door, and Dr. Saul came into his room. *Speaking of walking, talking medical charts.* "Afternoon, Jack. How are you feeling today?"

"Okay, Doc, except for the headaches. But no memories yet, and I'm starting to worry."

Setting his clipboard on the edge of the sink, Dr. Saul washed his hands then bent to examine Jack's bandage-wrapped head. "Well, son, it's as I told you, brain injuries are tricky things. As long as you're retaining new memories, just give it more time. The swelling in your head has gone down, and the MRI revealed no aneurysms. In most cases of retrograde amnesia, the memories eventually return. Sometimes in pieces. Sometimes all at once. With one or two holes, maybe, but nothing overly concerning."

"You sound encouraging." Jack sat up straighter in the bed. "That makes me feel better."

Dr. Saul clapped him on the shoulder. "You'll be fine. And I think we can safely remove this." Dr. Saul pulled off the tape and bandage. "The stitches look good, and you're healing nicely. You'll have a scar, but with your hair, no one will ever see it."

"Thanks, Dr. Saul. I appreciate you making sure my brains didn't ooze out."

"Ha. We always try to avoid oozing brains." He tossed the gauze into the biohazard trash container, then sat in the visitor chair and faced Jack. "Now, what's this I hear about you refusing to go to the Head Trauma Institute in Boise? Dr. Huber is tops in his field. He's already reviewed your case and is willing to take you without the benefit of insurance. The institute is state funded and has resident patients, which means while you recover, you won't have to worry about a place to live. It's a no-brainer, if you ask me."

Jack laughed. "I think I'm the no-brainer here."

Dr. Saul chuckled. "Poor choice of words, but don't let that detract from the soundness of my advice. While I have every expectation that you'll recover, head trauma is nothing to mess around with, especially in cases like yours. Go to Boise, Jack. Find out who you were. Who you *are*."

The doctor made complete sense. Of course, he did. Any reasonable person would heed his advice, but apparently Jack wasn't reasonable. *Good to know.* Besides, what possible reason could he give for not wanting to leave Jasper that didn't make him sound more unhinged than someone with amnesia?

And why hadn't he told Dr. Saul about the one memory he did have?

Marie Beaumont.

Every time he turned around, whether sleeping or awake, her image flashed before his eyes. Sometimes like a photo, flat and one-dimensional. Sometimes in motion. But in every instance, she appeared alone and fearful. And in every instance, she was a blonde.

"Look, Doc, I appreciate everything you've done for me. I mean that. But if I want to get my memories back, then Jasper is the place I need to be."

Dr. Saul perked up at this. "So you're remembering things, then? Something to do with Jasper?"

"Cool your jets, Doc. It's just a hunch, but it seems… well, it seems right somehow. I don't know how else to

explain it, other than my gut insists I should stay here."
So, how lame did that sound? He massaged his temples,
trying to ease the thundering drum solo in his head.

Dr. Saul *tsked* with resignation. "Suit yourself. I'll
order something for the headaches."

"Thank you." Jack smiled in relief. As long as he
had something for the pain, he could keep trying to
figure out his life.

Dr. Saul picked up his clipboard and scratched out
some quick notes. "Since you're determined not to go
to Boise, you need to understand something. With the
improvement in your physical condition, I'll have no
choice but to release you tomorrow. Have you at least
spoken to the hospital social worker? Figured out what
you're going to do, where you're going to go?"

He hadn't, but another rap on the open door saved
him from lying about it.

"Knock, knock." Jason stuck his head in. When he
saw the doctor, he said, "I can come back in a few minutes, if you need to finish up."

"No, we're done." The doctor turned back to Jack.
"If you're absolutely sure about not going to Boise,
promise me you'll speak to the social worker. Today."

"Ten-four, Doc."

The doctor's brows raised in doubt.

"I promise." Jack gave the doctor a genuine smile
and hoped the social worker could help him get a roof
over his head and a job. Without those, staying in Jasper would most likely be impossible.

"I'm holding you to that."

When he'd gone, Jason set a can of icy cold Coke

and a bag that smelled of carbohydrate heaven on the tray table. "Still no missing person reports that match your description, but I've widened the search area to include the surrounding states." Jason plopped into the visitor chair. "So, what was that about you not going to Boise?"

"Yeah, I've decided I like Jasper so much that I'm going to stay a while."

"And why's that?" Stretching his legs out, Jason yawned. "Is our small town helping your memory come back?"

"I wish." Jack chuckled at his wistful tone. "But I'm pretty sure if I stay here, it will. Thanks for the grub, by the way. I owe you, man." He unwrapped the burger Jason had brought him and bit off a huge chunk.

"Forget it." Jason stood and walked over to the window. "I find it interesting that a man who can't even remember his own name is suddenly an amnesia doctor."

Jack didn't take offense at the teasing sarcasm. "It's a hunch, okay?" He popped open the can of Coke and gulped half of it.

Jason shrugged. "A hunch, I understand. So, what did the doctor mean about a social worker?"

"It means I need to figure out where I'm going to live and how I'm going to pay for it when I get out of here. Tomorrow." Jack used his teeth to rip open a ketchup package, squeezed it out onto his burger wrapper, then dipped several warm, salty fries, darn near salivating in anticipation. *I should start keeping notes. I'm definitely a burger and fries man.* "Come to think about it, I probably owe a pile of cash to the hospital and Doc Saul." Jack popped the fries in his mouth and sighed with happiness. After swallowing, he continued, "In a nutshell, I'm broke and homeless."

"Oh, snap." Jason leaped from the chair. "I might have just the ticket. Need to make a call first. Back in a sec." And with that, he zipped out into the hallway.

Jack dragged another fry through the ketchup and chewed it as he pondered his situation. No name, no home, no past. But he was alive, saved by a beautiful woman. He had a new friend who was trying to find him a place to live. All in all, he was a very lucky man.

Now he just needed to fill in all the blanks.

Chapter Three

True to his word, Dr. Saul released Jack the next day. Because Jason's plan came through, Jack didn't even have to meet with the social worker. Seems a woman Jason knew, Emma Daniels, owned a spread north of town where she trained search and rescue dogs, and had horses there, as well. Ms. Daniels offered him room, board and a small stipend in exchange for his labor. She'd also promised to deduct from his wages the debt Jack was racking up. He'd insisted on that. Seems he didn't like owing people.

According to Jason, he'd be living in an RV while staying at Emma's, which had the added benefit of helping out some guy named Shane, whose girlfriend was mighty glad to get the monstrosity out of her driveway.

"Ready to blow this joint?" Once more, Jason was uniformed and ready to lend a hand. The young cop, who Jack owed a bigger debt than money could repay, would be going in to work after dropping Jack off. He scurried out of his police cruiser, which was parked in the circular drive in front of the hospital, and opened the passenger door.

"You have no idea." Dressed in a T-shirt, jeans and sneakers, which Jason had dropped off the day before, Jack waited while the nurse locked the wheelchair so he could stand.

"Then your chariot awaits."

Jack got in the car. He checked out the equipment console and comm system up front out of idle curiosity. He felt no connection to the squad car, but he couldn't deny a sense of déjà vu. Then he turned and looked through the steel mesh cage to the hard plastic seats in the back. A flash of memory came. Sitting in the back of a different squad car. Struggling with someone…a cop? The glint of handcuffs. A grunt of pain. Then it was gone.

Nausea hit Jack. Not from his persistent headache, but from wondering if he'd been that man. He tried to expand that brief flash of insight, but his head just throbbed in answer.

He buckled his seat belt as Jason got behind the wheel. "You're positive this is okay with your friend Emma? I mean, me staying on her property?"

Jason buckled up and started the car. "I told you, man. Everyone gave a thumbs-up."

"And they know about my condition? Heck, I could be an ax murderer, for all they know." The images flashed through his mind once more. "For all *I* know."

Well, maybe not a murderer. But possibly someone who belonged in the back of a cop car.

And that thought made him recall Marie's guarded reaction to him. Did she know more about him than he did? Maybe that he was some sort of criminal?

His head throbbed to the beat of his escalating heart rate.

Don't force it, Dr. Saul had told him.

Jack massaged his temples. *Easier said than done, Doc.*

Looking in his side mirror, Jason waited while a car pulled up alongside and double parked, boxing them in. "Trust me—Emma was all for it when I suggested you move out to the DCA. Of course, she'd already heard about your situation. Probably from Marie, who's out there all the time. Both of them were worried about where you'd wind up."

Jack adjusted the vent nearest him for a better blast of cool air. "You don't say."

So Marie was worried about him. He kind of liked that idea. Tons better than having her afraid of him. And maybe an indicator that she did not, in fact, have secret information about a nefarious past he couldn't remember.

They pulled away from the hospital into a cloudless morning with a wide sky, bluer than blue. The sun was cheerful and warm with the promise of real heat later in the day. An altogether gorgeous day Jack struggled to enjoy, because the glaring brightness had his head throbbing like a jackhammer.

As he and Jason drove through town, the Jasper PD officer pointed out various local landmarks. The town hall here, the police station there. The fire station, library, and at the intersection of Main and Elm, a picturesque town square complete with a gazebo.

They even drove by Marie's vet practice, which was

an old, converted house, the second floor an apartment where she lived.

He made note of that, just as he made note of the street names, the distance between buildings, the general layout of the town. Like he was mapping out escape routes. He noticed something else, too, when they stopped at the drug store where Jason fronted him the money to pay for his headache script.

At strategic points in the building were large round mirrors, and video cameras aimed at the checkout registers and pharmacy counter. Cameras Jack pegged as fakes, meant to scare off amateurs, except for the one in the back by the drugs. That camera not only filmed but stored it digitally without recording over it.

Jack frowned at the security camera, his fading headache now a solid drumbeat. How did he know that? *Why* did he know that?

Jack didn't like the first answer that came to him. The way he cataloged the entire security setup in less than twenty seconds felt like he was casing the joint.

About fifteen minutes later, they drove away from the pharmacy, Jack not even waiting for water before popping a pain pill, hoping it would settle the pounding in his head. "Thanks for these." He shook the pill bottle. "Add it to my tab?"

"Emma paid for them. She'll keep track of it and deduct it from your paycheck." Jason continued acting in the role of a Jasper tour guide. "There's Millard's Diner. That's where your burger came from yesterday, and a block down, over there is the Bartwell Brewing

Company. You ever come into town with an appetite, Millard's or Bartwell's are your best bets."

"I doubt I'll be coming into town very often."

"Oh? Why not?"

"No identity means no driver's license means no driving."

"Man, don't you know by now, I got your back?"

"Oh, yeah. And how's that?" Jack laughed. "A permission slip from the cops to drive without a license?"

Jason chuckled. "Wait and see."

As they headed north out of town, Jack tapped his fingers on his knees, impatient for the pill to work its magic. The brick and mortar of town gave way to rolling foothills, and he began to relax.

He'd learned something else while waiting in the pharmacy for his script to be filled. Something positive, for a change. Without thinking, he'd reached for a magazine and started flipping through the pages, barely looking at them. But then his attention focused, and his gut reacted in a way he was coming to recognize. Tightening, then relaxing, then growing a bit tingly with a sense of…familiarity, he supposed.

Holding up the magazine at the checkout, he'd asked Jason, "Mind if I add this to my tab?"

"Not at all. Rafting and kayaking, huh?"

Jack shrugged. "No flood of memories, if that's what you mean." But the images had certainly captured his attention, and he intended to go with his gut. What else did he have?

Eventually they turned onto a long dirt road, then drove under the framed entrance of the Daniels Canine

Academy, formed by two round posts and a wooden sign emblazoned with a German shepherd silhouette across the top. Jason parked in a large open area between a one-story white brick house and a small white barn.

Some distance from the barn sat the kennel, which was brown with a green roof that matched the one on the house. Even with the fenced runs along the sides of the kennel, there was enough room to park the RV between it and the barn.

"About time," called an attractive woman who came out from the barn, tugging off thick work gloves and then tucking them into the rear pocket of her well-worn jeans. Her light brown hair was pulled back, and as she approached, Jack noticed clear blue eyes that reminded him of Marie. Although, Emma's were light, like a cloudless summer sky. Marie's eyes were a much darker blue, more like a storm-tossed ocean.

"Hi. I'm Emma Daniels. You must be Jack."

"That's what they tell me." He smiled and shook her hand. "Appreciate you letting me stay here."

"Don't thank me yet. Earning your keep is going to be hard work. You're not afraid of hard work, are you, Jack?"

"I don't think so." He chuckled and rubbed the back of his neck, uneasy over being less than sure of himself. "Guess we'll find out together."

Her expression softened. "Tactless of me. Take no notice. As long as you give me a fair day's work, you can consider this your home until you're ready to move on. However long that might be." Emma gave him a friendly smile, but there was steel there, too. No push-over, this lady.

Turning her attention to Jason, she morphed into a mother role. "Shoo. Off to work with you. I got it from here."

"Yes, ma'am." Jason gave her a quick kiss on the cheek, then handed Jack the bag with his prescription and magazine. "Oh, I almost forgot." He pointed to where a serviceable old blue bicycle with a wire basket between the handlebars leaned against the side of the barn. "There's your transportation." He nudged Jack with his elbow, a smirk on his lips. "See, no license required."

Jack chuckled for the second time in less than five minutes. "I can deal with that. Thanks, man." Out of the sterile four walls of his hospital room and being offered a chance to move around and talk without medical supervision, he was starting to feel like his old self again.

Or what he hoped his old self felt like—relaxed and grateful.

"Protect and Serve. That's me." Then Jason headed out.

"He's a good boy," Emma remarked absently, watching Jason's disappearing cruiser with a faraway look. When the dust of his leaving settled, she snapped to. "One of my foster child success stories." She tilted her head in Jack's direction. "Hope you'll be one of my successes, too."

"Yes, ma'am."

"Well, come on, then. No time for dawdling. Before

I show you where you'll be working, let's get you set up in Shane's RV." She threw him a pleased look. "I think you'll be surprised."

She set off at a quick pace, and Jack trotted to catch up with her, each footfall sending a thread of pain up his spine and into his head, hot needles stabbing behind his eyes.

She halted before the RV door, unlocked it, then handed him the key. "Take care of this. I've got a spare, but I expect—" She stopped herself. "You'll have to forgive me. I'm used to dealing with teens, not full-grown men."

Jack smiled. "No apology necessary. I'll take good care of the key." He slid it into the coin pocket on his jeans.

Emma opened the door, and he followed her inside.

And surprised he was. The interior smelled new, the cabinets and furnishings extravagant, lavish even. If not for the fact it was so cramped that only a runway model could squeeze through, he might have called it perfect. "This is amazing." He'd get used to walking sideways.

Emma seemed to know what he was thinking. "Trust me. You'll fit. These buttons here work the slides."

In minutes, the slides opened up, expanding the living room by a good three feet. The bedroom opened up, as well. A good thing, since he wasn't exactly a small man. "Kitchen and bathroom are stocked. Bed's made up. Shane said you were to help yourself to the clothes until you can afford some of your own. He also asked that you keep the place clean and no smoking."

"Yes, ma'am. I'm pretty sure I didn't smoke before. And if I did, guess now's a good time to quit, right?" He followed her back to the front.

"For having your world turned upside down in an instant, you've got a good attitude." Emma laughed. "I hope everything here is acceptable to you."

"Totally acceptable. In fact, I can't thank you enough."

"You already have." Emma opened the door. "Dinner's at six at the house, and I imagine you'll have worked up an appetite by then. Just don't overdo, or Dr. Saul will have my hide. I'll give you a few minutes to catch your breath, then meet me in the kennel for your introduction to poop patrol." She winked at him. "Wear work boots. Shane left a pair for you in here, somewhere." And she was gone.

So far, so good. He'd wanted to stay in Jasper and here he was, in a luxury RV no less. He'd wanted to learn more about the pretty lady vet, and apparently she spent a lot of time here at the DCA.

Now he just needed to figure out his identity, why Jasper was so important to him and whether he was a good, or a very bad, person.

Hope for the best—prepare for the worst.

IT WAS ANOTHER warm sunny morning, three days after setting the broken leg of the stray. Raoul, a vet tech interning for Marie through a college program in Boise, had christened the dog Amaya. In her SUV, taking the recovering Amaya back to the DCA, Marie should have been engulfed in the warm-and-fuzzies.

She and Raoul had performed a near-miraculous surgery. The X-rays revealed a much worse break than Marie had originally thought. If the surgery hadn't been successful, the dog would have lost her leg. And if Emma hadn't found the poor thing and called Marie, Amaya and her pups would have died.

But worry overshadowed any sense of triumph. True, her two-legged stray, Jack, was long gone to Boise by now. But Deputy Murphy still hadn't returned her multiple calls and texts. What if Jack really was a threat to her and had stayed in Jasper, making her emergency real and immediate? What then? Murphy had never failed to respond when she'd reached out in the past. Something must be wrong. And not knowing scared Marie like she hadn't been scared since…since the last time she'd seen Abel Gaines.

Sensing her distress, Astrid woofed. "You're right, girl. Nothing I can do right this minute." But Marie wondered if maybe she shouldn't just drive to Boise and find out what was going on for herself.

Shutting off the engine, she worked to shed her anxiety. "Come on, Astrid." She climbed out of the SUV and Astrid hopped out right behind her, following Marie around to the back. Opening the hatch, she left the carrier in the car, opting instead to carry the dog. "Here we are, Amaya. Home sweet home." She hefted the pregnant stray into her arms and strode toward the kennel.

Stepping into the kennel's cool, dark interior brought

instant relief from the sun's heat. The impatient dog struggled to get down. "Knock it off, Amaya. I'm trying to help you here."

"Need a hand?"

Marie froze. Her mouth went dry, and her heart rate ratcheted up. Astrid drew near, ears twitching and tail up, stance alert.

Turning in a slow spin, Marie peered through the gloom. "Jack?"

About ten feet away, his shadowy form leaned on a shovel handle. "DCA poop patrol, at your service."

Based on his words and light tone, he meant to be funny. But nothing about this situation struck Marie as the least bit amusing. "What are you doing here?" Her words carried a sharp edge. "I thought you were going to Boise."

"I was. Plans changed. And at the moment, I'm cleaning the kennels. Why don't you let me help you get that dog settled?"

"Her name is Amaya, and I can manage."

Think, Marie, think.

A stranger who had shown up a few days ago out of nowhere, supposedly with no memory, standing in Emma's kennel instead of a hospital in Boise. At the same time that Deputy US Marshal George Murphy had suddenly gone AWOL. Coincidence? Maybe. If you believed in them. And Marie did not.

Sensing her mistress's concern, Astrid stayed by her side as Marie walked to the last stall, bent her knees and set Amaya down. The poor stray didn't seem at all happy about being forced into the small pen Emma had prepared in order to limit her movement. But then, being forced to endure things one didn't like happened to everyone from time to time.

"Just for a little while, girl." Marie calmed Amaya, then stood and did a quick search for a weapon just in case she needed one. The only thing available was a metal dog bowl. Not nearly as effective as her pepper spray, which she had conveniently left in her car.

Stupid, stupid, stupid.

Well, if it came to it, Astrid was trained to attack if Marie gave the command.

Her eyes had adjusted to the dim lighting of the kennel enough to see tousled brown hair brushing against impossibly broad shoulders. The white T-shirt he wore stretched tight across his chest and showed off arms defined by corded muscles. An unlikely mixture of tempered fear and cautious pleasure filled her. He was a pretty one, all right. But Abel had been pretty, too.

Jack had put down the shovel and moved closer. Marie tensed.

He must have sensed her discomfort. "Have I done something to offend you?"

If he'd come here to kill her, he would have already. Unless he really did have amnesia and forgot he was supposed to kill her. In which case, each recovered memory of his might bring her one memory closer to death. She gave herself a mental eye roll. Until she spoke to George, all she could do was try to figure out Jack's identity while working to get him out of Jasper. Out of her life.

"No, I'm just tired." The lie came easily. Well, it wasn't as if she hadn't had plenty of practice.

"What happened to her?" Jack asked, indicating Amaya.

"We think she was tossed from a moving vehicle during the storm. Broken leg, road rash all over and she's pregnant. Not to mention quite a few old scars."

"That's rough. She going to be okay?"

His concern seemed genuine. But she wasn't exactly the best judge of men, or the validity of emotions they expressed. "Should be, but I can't be sure about the puppies."

"When's she due?"

"Any day now. That's why I wanted to get her back here so fast."

"So, she came out of the same storm as me?"

"Apparently so."

Jack squatted and looked Astrid in the eyes. "And who is this beauty?"

"Her name is Astrid. She's the one who helped me get you out of the culvert." And Astrid was an excellent judge of character.

She gave the dog a slight tap, releasing her from Marie's side. Astrid woofed in pleasure and, tail wagging, went up to Jack and sniffed him. He remained still, his hand extended, and Astrid, the little traitor, licked his palm.

Then Jack did something unexpected. Something Marie had seen Emma, a professional trainer, do countless times. He slapped the flat of his hand against his chest in invitation. Astrid responded by jumping up on two legs, front paws planted on his shoulders.

Jack laughed, a rich, warm baritone sound. A genuine laugh. He ruffled Astrid's ears. "Nice to meet you, too."

Marie couldn't help but smile. "Astrid, down."

"She's definitely well-behaved. Was she trained here?"

Marie nodded. "As an attack dog." *Just putting that out there in case you get any ideas, buster.*

"Really?" Jack scratched Astrid's tummy, now that she was stretched out on the floor. "A lot of crime in Jasper?"

"No more or less than any other place." Marie checked Amaya's bowls for fresh water and food. "So why aren't you in Boise trying to sort out this memory loss thing?"

"Decided I'd rather stay here. As odd as it sounds, my gut's telling me that if I want my memories back, I need to be in Jasper. And thanks to Jason, Emma was kind enough to offer me a place to stay." He nodded in the direction of the shovel. "And a job. Cleaning kennels isn't much, but when you're broke, it's everything." He shrugged, the movement doing great things for his shoulders. "So, here I am. Thanks to a lot of nice people in this town."

Marie blinked to keep from reacting to the heart-stopping smile on Jack's face. "Yeah, Jasper is great like that."

The kennel's atmosphere changed in a flash, as if an electrical current whipped through the room. Jack stared at her again with that all-knowing intensity she remembered from the side of the road.

"Marie?"

She swallowed. Her pulse stuttered. "What?"

"Thank you." He ducked his head, then raised his eyes to meet hers. "For saving my life."

She let out a silent sigh of relief. "No thanks necessary."

"You say that like it was nothing." He straightened to a standing position, and Astrid followed his cue. "But it wasn't nothing. It was my life." He beat a fist against his chest one time, his voice breaking with emotion. "I can never repay you for that. But I'd like to try. For starters, maybe you'll let me take you to dinner?"

Marie appreciated his gratitude, but going to dinner together? Not gonna happen. "Thought you were broke." She tempered her words with a teasing tone.

"We might have to wait a couple weeks while I save up my allowance." He gave her a mischievous grin that took her breath away.

As her guard around Jack began to slip a little and her attraction to him grew, it would still be best to nip this in the bud. *Remember Abel.* Even if Jack hadn't been sent to kill her, he was dangerous to her self-control.

"Not to worry. No repayment needed." She latched the door on Amaya's stall. "But maybe you can answer a question for me."

"I'll try, but lately I seem to have more questions than answers, myself."

She crossed her arms over her chest. "That first day in the hospital, you asked me if I'd been a blonde. Why?"

"I'm not sure. I guess you must look like someone I know who's blonde, but I have no idea who." He shrugged. "*Did* you used to be blonde?"

Marie ignored his question but considered his answer. It could be the case, but how would she know if he was lying? "Well, have fun on poop patrol. I've gotta go. I need to take a look at Elton's hoof." Her voice came out in a rush, and she hustled from the kennel, calling Astrid to her side. She had to get rid of him, and she had to do it now. To accomplish that, she would need Emma's help.

She found Emma sweeping the central area in the barn. "There you are."

"Marie, watch out." Emma motioned her out of the way as she sprinkled water on the floor and swept dust into a pile. "You bring my stray back?"

"I did. And by the way, her name's Amaya."

Emma snickered. "Amaya, huh? Let me guess. Raoul?"

"Of course." Marie chuckled. "It means night rain in Basque."

"Aw, I like that." Emma's face softened. "Fits her perfectly. Is she settled in? Was the pen what you needed?"

"Yes, and yes." Marie looked around the empty barn. "Um, I thought I was going to check Elton's hoof today."

"Darn it." Emma stopped sweeping and slapped a

palm to her forehead. "I completely forgot. Hugh and Kyle came out today to work, but I already had Jack mucking stalls and scooping the paddock. They asked if they could exercise the horses instead, and Elton didn't seem to be favoring that foot. I thought maybe I'd just imagined him limping."

Hugh, Kyle and William worked afternoons and weekends for Emma through a co-op program for at-risk kids at the local high school. Wanting to make sure they also stayed out of trouble during the summer, Emma offered them part-time jobs.

"Tell you what. I have a light day at the clinic tomorrow, so I'll just come back in the morning and take a look. I'd rather catch it early, if he does have something wrong."

"Perfect. Thanks." Emma went back to her sweeping.

Marie perched on a bale of hay and tried to keep her tone neutral. "You want to tell me how Jack ended up here?"

Emma's broom froze midsweep. She straightened her back and met Marie's questioning look with one of resolve. "He needed a place to stay and a way to earn some money. I can never have too much help. Figured it was a win-win situation." Her lips curled into a sly smile. "Besides, I thought you might appreciate having him around. You seemed quite taken with him, and girl, you weren't exaggerating about him being good-looking."

"I'm not taken with him, or anybody else for that matter." Marie crossed her arms to emphasize her denial. "In fact, I think you should send him to Boise. There's a brain trauma specialist there willing to take him without insurance. He'd have a place to stay, and money wouldn't be an issue. Dr. Saul is really worried about him. By giving him a place to stay here, you're not helping him. You could be hurting him."

Emma shook her head. "Give me a little credit. I spoke to Dr. Saul before making the offer to Jack. True, he doesn't agree with Jack's decision to stay here, but he doesn't think it will harm him, either."

"And what if he ends up being some serial killer? I get strange vibes from him. I'm telling you—you're not safe with him here."

"'Methinks the lady doth protest too much.'" Emma's words came out in a singsong version of a bad English accent.

Marie stood. "What are you talking about?"

"If I didn't know better, I'd think you have a crush on him." Emma sprayed more water on the floor. "Not that I'd blame you."

"Oh, please." But Marie's heart sank. Emma would not be her ally in this. If she was going to get rid of Jack, she'd have to come up with Plan B.

"You know," Emma went on, "it wouldn't kill you to have a social life."

You never know, Emma. It actually might.

JACK MAY BE missing most of his memories, but reading people seemed to come easily to him. Doc Saul, Jason, Emma—piece of cake. But Marie? She was the proverbial onion with lots of layers. Jack stood outside the kennel, following her progress as she practically ran to the barn to find Emma. But he couldn't tell if she was running to Emma or away from him.

What reason did she have to act so skittish around him? True, he was a man from nowhere with nothing, not even a name. But no one else seemed bothered by that. She actually appeared to be afraid of him, and that rankled.

The first time he met her, in the hospital, she'd been touted as his savior. So when he was unconscious, she had no problem saving his life. But awake, he apparently seemed poised to leap from his bed and bite her head off.

Today, she came into the kennel happy and talking to dogs, until the moment she'd become aware of his presence. Then she'd gone all starchy and hard. He'd even maintained a safe distance, spoken in soft, non-threatening tones, even made a joke. She might have even been softening, but then, like a bolt of lightning, she'd practically run out of the kennel as if fleeing the hounds of hell.

One minute friendly, the next wanting nothing to do with him. Not that he blamed her, entirely. She'd found him in a muddy ditch. And now he was mucking horse stalls and shoveling dog runs for a living. He was not a catch for the sexy vet. He got that. But someone to fear?

Marie Beaumont—a woman with wintry blue eyes and full, ever-so-kissable lips. A woman with dark hair who haunted him as a blonde. A woman who championed strays but didn't always trust them.

Marie Beaumont made his head hurt.

Despite that, he was inexplicably drawn to her. Not just sexually attracted, though there was that. He wanted to know everything about her. As much as he hankered to unearth his own past, he wanted to discover hers even more.

He finished up the last of his indoor kennel chores, cleaned the shovel, then grabbed a muck rake and started for the paddock on the far side of the barn. He stopped short when Marie went speed-walking from the barn to her vehicle, Astrid right on her heels. Jack's gaze followed the trail of dust left by her speeding SUV as she drove away down the dirt road.

And that sudden, razor-sharp pain struck him with an intensity so powerful, he bent double and grabbed his head in both hands. Behind his eyes he saw another trail of dust, from another time, another place. A place thick with trees. Men shouting. The *pop, pop, pop* of automatic gunfire. He flinched and bucked as if dodging live bullets. Then his wrist was on fire, the burning pain overshadowing the pain in his head.

In the next instant, his mind went dark, and the horror-filled memories retreated back behind the walls of his amnesia. He panted, trying to catch his breath. Cool, clammy sweat covered his skin. He straightened, massaging his temples, checking his body for bullet holes he knew weren't there. Examining his left arm, he stopped cold. Thick, fibrous ridges and slick indentations covered the wrist and forearm. Burn scars.

All this time, he'd assumed the undercurrent of danger he sensed when he was around Marie had something to do with her. But now, with these memories, maybe he was the one in trouble.

"Oh my gosh, Jack. You look pale as a ghost. You okay?" Piper Lambert, a dog trainer at DCA, stood in the kennel doorway. A tall woman with long dark red hair, her green eyes reflected genuine concern. She had a harnessed dog, her latest search and rescue trainee, on one side. On her other side was a corgi mix puppy she'd adopted recently. It was kind of cool that every day at the DCA was *Bring Your Pet to Work* day.

"Just another one of my headaches," Jack assured her. "It's already passed."

"I don't happen to think it was just another one of your headaches. You should see yourself. Sit, will you? Before you fall."

He dropped onto a nearby bench.

"That's better. Do I need to call Emma, or maybe Dr. Saul?"

"Absolutely not." They might send him to Boise. He needed to stay in Jasper. He had to give Piper something to make her back down. "Okay, you got me. It wasn't just another headache. I got a flash of memory."

She gave him a broad smile. "That's outstanding. Can you remember your name? Who you are?"

"Nothing like that, unfortunately. Just a dirt road. Some trees. Well, lots of trees. Nothing I recognized." He swallowed that half-truth he'd just told. "No big deal, really."

"Of course, it's a big deal. Wait until I tell—"

"Do you mind not saying anything about this? Not

yet anyway. I want to tell people in my own time. You know, once I get my head wrapped around it."

"Sorry, I wasn't thinking." She dropped her gaze. "Of course. I won't say anything."

And despite only meeting Piper a few days ago, Jack believed her.

"Thanks." That's when he looked down. Muddy boot steps and equally muddy paw prints crisscrossed the concrete floor he'd just washed. He blew out an exasperated breath.

Piper snickered. "Sorry about that, but you might as well get used to it. It's a never-ending job." She ushered her trainee into one of the stalls, removed its harness and gave the water dish a quick look. "At least you remember to clean and fill their bowls. The after-school kids took a while to learn that one."

"After-school kids?"

"Yeah, there're three of them this year. Hugh, Kyle and William. Have you met them yet?"

"No, but I saw two teenage boys earlier. They disappeared into the barn."

"That would be Hugh and Kyle. They're out exercising the horses right now." Her mouth screwed up into a droll smile. "I bet they were *so* disappointed to find out you've taken over as head poop scooper."

Jack chuckled. "It's a crappy job, but someone has to do it."

Piper planted her hands on her hips in a battle stance. "I like your can-do-doo attitude."

Jack held up his hands in surrender, chuckling. "Enough. You win."

He'd met Piper when he first arrived at DCA, but they hadn't had much of a chance to chat it up yet. With well-practiced ease, she hung the harness on the wall and crossed her arms, studying Jack as she might a dog about to become a new trainee. "You settling in okay?"

Jack waggled his hand from side to side in a so-so gesture. "I could be doing a lot worse. I really appreciate you and Shane letting me use your RV."

"Technically, it's just Shane's. And I should be thanking you. At first, I loved it when he parked that huge thing in my driveway, because I knew it meant he was staying." She shrugged. "But after almost four months, I'm so ready to have my driveway back."

"Glad I could help out." Like some nervous tick, Jack scuffed his boot against the floor. "It's been nice getting to know folks around here. Marie just left." *Smooth, Jack, real smooth.*

"Yeah, I saw her tear out when I was coming in. Probably some clinic emergency. That gal loves animals, which is saying a lot around here. She told me once that from the time she was a little girl, she felt a calling to heal injured critters."

"I guess you know her pretty well, then?"

Piper shrugged again. "As well as anyone, I suppose. Nice as they come, but she doesn't open up much." Amaya whined, and Piper ambled down to the last stall.

Hoping to learn something, anything, about the enigmatic Marie, Jack followed her. "Why is that?"

"Who knows?" Piper opened the stall door and crossed to Amaya's pen. "And to be honest, I don't need to know about someone's past in order to like them for who they are now. Or not like them, as the case may be."

"Glad you feel that way. Otherwise, there'd be no chance for me."

Crouching down, Piper reached in and rubbed Amaya's head. "Hey, with me, you're in until you're out. But with Marie? Well, you best count on being in the getting-to-know-you category for quite some time."

"Gives me something to strive for. Full acceptance in Jasper, Idaho." He left the stall, refilled the bucket with water and grabbed the mop, ready to clean up the muddy footprints after Piper left.

Piper laughed. "We're generally not a tough crowd. I'm sure you'll fit in just fine." She leaned toward him and stage-whispered, "Unless the law's after you. You're not the leader of some fringe group hiding out in the hills, are you?" She hooked a thumb over her shoulder. "Ruby Ridge is just up the road, you know." With a wink and another laugh, she headed out the door.

And just like that, Jack knew Ruby Ridge. In Boundary County, Idaho. Site of an eleven-day siege in 1992. Three people dead, including one deputy US marshal. Of all the things to remember, and with such clarity and detail.

He shook his head. Bizarre. And even more bizarre, the memory had returned without pain. When that standoff happened, Jack was pretty young. It wasn't a true memory, but something he'd learned from a book or TV.

His stomach cramped into a cold ball of dread. The mention of Ruby Ridge triggered a recall of something learned, just minutes after a dusty dirt road triggered a painful flash of true memories. Memories of gunshots and burns. There had to be a connection.

But the connection was far from clear, and as Jack struggled to find it, his headache returned in earnest.

Chapter Four

After practically fleeing the DCA, Marie eased up on the gas pedal. She tapped her hands-free console and rang George Murphy. Still no answer. No point in leaving another message. Frustrated at not being in control of her own life, she opted for routine and called her office.

"Anything I need to come in for?" Marie asked her office manager through the car's speaker phone.

Liz Jellis had worked for a small law firm in Jasper until a car full of partying tourists mowed her down as she crossed the street on her lunch hour. Multiple surgeries later, her right leg had more metal than bone. Her boss sued the driver on her behalf, handed Liz her share of the settlement and promptly retired for parts unknown.

A few years later, her settlement money gone and still without a job, Liz had brought in her sick cat right at closing time. Marie, who could never say no to an ill or injured animal, had invited Liz in after hours. After hearing the woman's story, she'd treated her beloved tabby at no cost and hired Liz on the spot, never once regretting it.

"Nothing you need to be here for, but aren't you supposed to be working on Elton?"

"I was, but there was a mix-up. If my schedule's clear, I plan to go back tomorrow." Marie tried to ignore the sudden cramp twisting her stomach.

"Let's see. You have a couple appointments in the afternoon, but tomorrow morning is free."

"Great. And what about my schedule for the rest of today?"

"Free and clear." Liz's tone turned serious. "And you shouldn't sound so happy about that. You have some pretty big bills coming in."

"Don't I always make bills?"

"You do, but I would be remiss if I didn't remind you. Where are you off to?"

"To pick up some fudge, and then I'm heading over to Hemlock Hills. I haven't seen Dotty all week."

"Then you better get on over there. And tell her I said hi, will you?"

"You bet."

"I'll never understand why they named that place after hemlock, even if it *is* for the *non*-poisonous trees nearby." Liz scoffed. "Every time I hear it, reminds me of 'Hotel California' by the Eagles. You know, the part about checking out but not leaving."

Marie chuckled. "Well, that's a bit morbid, but the residents don't seem to mind. They even joke about it."

"Oh, don't forget the fundraiser at Bartwell's Friday night."

"Got it on my calendar. See you tomorrow."

TAKING A DEEP, cleansing breath, Marie inhaled the hint of fresh lavender as soon as she and Astrid walked into the airy, sunlit foyer of Hemlock Hills. The staff here had no need for plug-in scent diffusers meant to hide the stench of bodily functions, nor did they use that eye-watering pine cleanser that made everything stink like a morgue. No, Hemlock Hills was a far cry from the corporate-run facility where her grandmother had spent her final days.

After Marie had been orphaned in a car crash at the age of three, Granny Mae had raised her. As an adult, Marie had cared for her grandmother when cancer ravaged her body. Since she was an immediate family member, Granny Mae could have accompanied Marie into witness protection. But her grandmother had been too sick to travel, and insisted she'd be just fine in a nursing home. And the woman Marie owed everything to had died alone with no one to mourn her. Marie's guilt over leaving her grandmother behind was something she grappled with every day. But her friendship with Dotty helped salve the pain.

"Hi, Dr. Beaumont." Kim, the young woman who manned the reception desk, smiled. "Miss Dotty has been asking after you and Astrid."

"Oh, no. She's not mad enough to throw anything at me, is she?"

Kim snickered. "You go on in and let me know."

"Coward."

Marie hurried through the large family room with plump couches, shelves packed with books and a large-screen TV quietly broadcasting the news. At a table next to a large window, four women sat playing bridge. They exchanged waves with Marie, then returned to their game.

The Hills, as it was sometimes called, was a sprawling one-story ranch-style home on the northern edge of town. It had been converted into an assisted living facility with ten small private rooms. Not long after moving to Jasper, Marie had been called to the Hills about a stray cat. Seemed the residents had fallen in love with Sassy Cat, as she came to be known, and asked to adopt her. The only way the owner would agree was if the cat was current on shots and rendered sterile.

As always, Astrid accompanied Marie during the back and forth with Sassy Cat and became an instant favorite of the feisty older woman in 5A, Dotty Hazzard. And Dotty Hazzard became an instant favorite of Marie's, filling the gaping hole left by her grandmother's passing.

Marie knocked.

"That better be Astrid and her never-comes-to-see-old-Dotty-anymore owner. Well, come on in here before I croak."

Marie opened the door of the cheerful space and released Astrid just as Dotty hit Mute on *Judge Judy*. Astrid went straight to the easy chair where Dotty sat and laid her head in the woman's lap. Dotty's collection of bangle bracelets jingled on both arms as she scratched and petted and cooed. "Here's my good girl. At least *you* love me, don't you, Astrid?"

Marie perched on the tie-dye quilt on Dotty's bed. Each resident was allowed to decorate their room however they wished, and Dotty, an original flower child, Woodstock attendee and once-upon-a-time commune resident, had gone full-on hippie, bohemian in her decor. Colorful batik hangings covered the walls, rattan chairs with bright cushions sat on a paisley rug and plants hung in macramé holders.

The lady herself wore her long gray hair in twin braids and got scolded on a regular basis for playing her classic rock favorites too loud. "Fetch me the jar, hon."

No need to specify which one. Marie got up and reached for the dog biscuit container, a purple glass jar hand-painted with a gold Moroccan design. She handed the jar to Dotty, who unscrewed the lid, and soon Astrid was chomping away.

Dotty put the lid back on and squeezed the jar onto the side table next to her that also held her TV remote, tissue box, one pill bottle and a glass of lemonade. "So, life must be keeping you real busy these days."

Smiling at Dotty's rebuke, Marie dropped into the chair next to her, sinking into the pink-and-orange cushions with a grateful sigh. "It has, actually." She pulled the scrunchie off her ponytail and sighed again when her hair fell around her face. "The morning after that big storm we had last week, Astrid and I went jogging as usual, and I found a guy along the side of the road. Well, Astrid found him."

Dotty leaned forward, rubbing her arthritic hands together. "Was he murdered?"

"What?" Marie's shock at the old lady's morbid excitement made her voice louder than usual. "No."

"Oh." Disappointment colored Dotty's tone. "I

thought maybe we'd have an intriguing mystery to solve. Something to activate the old brain cells."

"I think you've been watching too many true crime shows."

Dotty waved off Marie's suggestion. "Okay, okay. So he wasn't murdered." She folded her arms across where her breasts used to be. Burning her bra decades ago, along with the undeniable force of gravity, had relocated them somewhere between her sternum and her belly button. "Was he at least dead?"

Marie rolled her eyes. "I called 911, and they took him to the hospital."

"Is that all?" Dotty complained with a phony pout. "I can see where *you* might consider that mildly newsworthy, you being so young and lacking any real-life experience, but it's hardly reason enough for not visiting me. Anything else?"

"Actually, there is. I think he might be—" Marie caught herself. It was too easy to relax around Dotty.

"He might be, what?" Dotty probed.

"Well, he hit his head pretty hard. That's why he was unconscious. When he woke up, he couldn't remember anything about his past. Retrograde amnesia, his doctor called it."

"Go on with you now. His name wouldn't happen to be Jason Bourne, would it?"

"Ha-ha. Very funny. His name is Jack." Marie shrugged. "Least, we think it is. And for your information, he doesn't look anything at all like Matt Damon, if that's what you were fishing for."

"So what *does* he look like?"

Marie fiddled with the fringe on one of the throw pillows. "Handsome, I suppose, when his face isn't covered with mud."

"Uh-huh."

Marie didn't need to meet Dotty's eyes to know she was getting a thorough once-over.

"So tell me what your plans are for this handsome guy you found in a ditch. Not the usual way to meet men, but hey, if it works, more power to you."

"I have no plans for him." Marie forced herself to stop pulling on the pillow tassel before she yanked it right off.

"Don't pass up this chance, kiddo. You saved the life of a hunk, and now he owes you. I say take him home and keep him." She slapped her hand on her thigh and cackled. When Marie didn't bite, Dotty's playfulness fell away and her tone grew serious. "Oh, come on. Face it, sweetheart. You need a man in the worst kind of way. Far as I know, you haven't had one since you hit town. It ain't right for a woman your age to be alone."

"I have Astrid. Besides, my life is just fine as it is." Sometimes, she really did miss having a man around. What she didn't miss was the anxiety that came with them.

"No offense to Astrid, but a dog isn't a man. Look at me." Marie flicked her gaze up, and Dotty leaned forward, resting her hand on Marie's arm. "Maybe a man who can't remember his past is perfect for a woman trying to forget hers. Maybe you should try not to worry so much about who he used to be and just get to know the man he is now."

"I'm not sure I can do that. Besides, I don't have the best track record when it comes to judging men."

Sitting back in her chair, Dotty shifted around until she seemed comfortable. "So, tell me more about this Jack."

Marie filled Dotty in, careful to keep to the facts.

"And so now he's staying in Shane's RV out at the DCA, and you don't like it."

"I never said I didn't like it."

"Well, your face surely did. What is it about this Jack that you don't like?"

Marie stiffened, and like a pressure cooker, all her pent-up fear bubbled to the surface. "I don't like that he came out of nowhere. I don't like that everyone seems to trust him without knowing a single thing about him. I don't like that he refused to go to Boise and be treated, for free I might add, by a head trauma specialist because his gut tells him he should stay in Jasper. A place, incidentally, where not one person knows him."

Eyebrows high and forehead wrinkles deep, Dotty stared at her. "Feel better now?"

A laugh erupted from Marie. "Actually, I do."

"Always a good thing, getting that stuff off your chest. Want to get high?"

"Dotty." Marie swatted her friend's leg with the pillow she still held.

Dotty doubled over, laughing. "Ah, you know I was only pulling your leg."

"You're incorrigible." Marie laughed along with her, knowing the old woman loved that joke.

"It's what keeps me young." Dotty's expression

turned somber. "You know, sweetheart, I doubt this Jack is someone to worry about. But don't forget that half the police force is out at the DCA a lot, what with their dogs being trained and all. In a pinch, those high school kids are out there, too."

Astrid moved beside Marie and butted her head against Marie's knee until she got a dog biscuit.

"And even you've said so yourself, Emma is an excellent judge of character. But I get you. You have a hard time with things that aren't neat and tidy. And you think this man Jack is about as messy as they come." Dotty opened a container of breath mints and shook one out, then passed them to Marie. "Just see how it goes, and if he does anything that scares you, you report it. Okay?"

"Okay," Marie lied.

Dotty hmphed. "This has something to do with your past, doesn't it? That dark place you never talk about."

"It does, and I'll work through it like I always do." Marie straightened her spine, refusing to let this get her down. "Talking to you helps."

"Well, I'm glad to hear it, although I'm not sure how. No one should go through this life alone, kiddo. You got to have someone to talk to. And laugh with. Someone to help you get those doggone fitted sheets onto your mattress." She drained her lemonade. "Now then, what's going on at Bartwell's this weekend? I heard they're having some sort of special social thing."

Glad to be back on safe ground, Marie jumped on the topic. "One of the brewery's seasonal employees, I think her name's Millie, was diagnosed with cancer and she doesn't have insurance. The Bartwells decided to host barbecues once a week and donate the proceeds to offset her skyrocketing medical bills."

"Good people, the Bartwells. They always look out for their employees. Are you going?"

"I'm thinking about it. Do you want to go with me?"

"Nah, but thanks for asking. I'll probably be asleep by the time the dancing starts."

"Oh, I almost forgot." Marie rummaged in her bag. "I brought you some fudge."

"You know me so well. Thanks, kiddo."

"Now, what about *your* news? I thought you were working on the mystery of the missing clothes." Apparently, some items had gone into the laundry room, never to be seen again.

"Oh, shoot. I forgot to tell you." A satisfied smile spread across Dotty's face. "We solved it."

"We?"

Dotty nodded. "We. Us. The ones with the missing clothes."

"Well, don't keep me in suspense. Who's the culprit?"

"Betty Turnbull." Dotty rolled her eyes. "She showed up at movie night wearing Edith's blouse and my shawl, then claimed it was an accident. Can you believe the gall?"

Marie closed her eyes, a running profile of the female residents filtering through her mind. "Which one is Betty?"

"She's new. You haven't met her yet. She's the one I told you about who eats the fresh rose on her table every night at dinner. And then picks her teeth with the thorn." With an indelicate grunt, Dotty pushed up from her chair. "They must get those flowers awful cheap, 'cause the stems *always* have thorns. Come on—let's walk and talk. Every time I sit too long, I get stiff."

Dotty's limp was more pronounced than usual and her gait slow as they wandered into the family room, where the TV news droned on and the Hemlock Four, as Dotty called them, were still at their game of bridge. Across the room, near the large fireplace, sat a drink station with coffee, iced tea, lemonade and water.

Marie couldn't miss Dotty's grimaces during the short distance they'd walked. "Why don't you sit, and I'll get you more lemonade." She set her bag on the couch and told Astrid to stay.

"You're too good to me." With a grateful sigh, Dotty edged down on one of the couches and took the glass of cold lemonade when Marie brought it over.

After taking a long draw on the sweet drink, she smacked her lips. "Stay 'til the news is over?"

The plea tugged at Marie's heart. "Watching the news with you is one of my favorite things to do."

"I don't believe you, but I'll let you lie to me about it." Dotty reached for the remote and turned up the volume, waiting for the commercials to be over. "Dang lemonade. I need to use the can."

"Charming as ever." Marie chuckled as she rose to help Dotty get to her feet.

After that, Dotty swatted her away. "I got it from here." She shuffled toward the restroom near the lobby.

With nothing to do but wait, Marie turned to the TV when the news anchor announced a breaking alert.

"In a daring early morning escape, survivalist Abel Gaines escaped the US Penitentiary, Hazelton in West Virginia…"

At the name Abel Gaines, everything went cold. At the word *escape*, the nursing home faded from view as shock hit her. Abel's face, his mug shot, stared back at her from the screen.

No, no, no. Astrid whined, and Marie realized she'd spoken out loud.

Marie curled in on herself. She wrapped her arms across her churning stomach, barely noticing her icy hands as they cupped her elbows.

"…serving multiple life sentences for the deaths of five civilians and FBI Agent Mike Winston. Convicted as a domestic terrorist, Gaines was also charged with treason when plans to blow up several federal government buildings were discovered along with an arsenal of small arms and a cache of C-4 explosives."

Astrid nuzzled into her, the dog's stable heartbeat and warmth grounding her enough to catch the rest of what the news was saying.

"Gaines reportedly killed one prison guard and seriously wounded another during the escape. It's believed he was assisted by at least one of his original co-conspirators, and unconfirmed sources in the FBI say it's most likely his older brother Seth Gaines. The youngest Gaines brother, Isaac, was killed during the shootout five years ago when several law enforcement agencies attempted to serve arrest warrants at the Gaines family compound in the Allegheny Mountains. Gains was reportedly seen fleeing west, so the manhunt has expanded to include Ohio and Kentucky. More news as—"

A high-pitched buzz in Marie's ears drowned out the TV, and her gaze darted around the room, each item it touched coming in and out of focus like a drug-induced hallucination.

Dotty materialized in front of her. "Why, honey, you look like you've seen a ghost."

I have.

Marie parted her lips to speak, but her mouth seemed filled with cotton. She reached for her lemonade and drained the glass. "I…it's nothing." Standing, she grabbed her bag and Astrid's harness. "I know I promised, but I really need to go. I feel a stomach bug coming on."

"Go on, then. Take care of yourself." Dotty lowered herself onto the couch. "Keep me posted on your fella. And if you're still unsure about him, bring him by. Let me get a feel for him."

"Will do. See you soon." Marie kissed the top of Dotty's head, then for the second time that day, forced herself to walk, not run, to her car.

Abel Gains escaped. George Murphy was MIA. The unexpected arrival of Jack, who just happened to have no memory.

After turning the ignition key and locking the doors, Marie pulled out her phone and jabbed her case deputy's number for the umpteenth time. Instead of hearing his gravelly voice, a female recording informed her that this number was no longer in service. She slammed the phone down on the center console.

Fine. She would handle this herself.

Chapter Five

Dirt road. Dust flying up. Lush green trees. Maple, poplar, ash. Rolling hills. Afternoon sun. Heat. An idyllic scene that was anything but.

Blue-and-red flashing lights. Law enforcement. Uniforms everywhere. A barrage of gunfire. Handguns. Semiautomatics. The thwunk *from a tear gas canister. Trailing white smoke. Shouting. Men running. More shots. More shouting.*

A room, small, rustic, messy. Windows barricaded. Shell casings littering the floor. Sunlit dust motes. Still bodies. Sightless eyes. Blood everywhere. On the floor, the walls. On the living. The dead.

Flames raced along the dry wood siding of a building. A hand reached out. Fighting. Voices yelling. A body.

Pain blacked out the scene.

Jack bolted upright in bed, gasping for breath. As the horror show faded, he struggled to get his bearings. Bedroom. Shane's RV. The DCA. Marie.

Angry, confused and drenched in sweat, Jack flipped away the sheets and headed to the cramped bathroom. Cupping water from the faucet, he splashed his face then scooped a handful into his parched mouth, slushed it around, spit it out. A foul taste still lingered.

He brushed his teeth, looking at himself in the mirror. Was the face he stared at the face of a killer? What he'd experienced in his sleep, what he remembered now that he was awake, was a whole lot of death. He winced. Even his head was killing him. He reached for his pill bottle, shook one out and swallowed.

Flipping on the shower, he stepped in without waiting for the water to warm. He hoped the icy needles of water would help drive away the pictures in his mind. Just as he had every morning since moving to the DCA.

What Jack had seen was nothing he'd learned about from a book or on TV. He was remembering. The pain in his head confirmed that. The images were spotty and incomplete, but he recalled the verdant smell of the trees, the metallic stench of blood as he walked among the corpses.

The skylight above him displayed a bright, cloudless sky. But the sunny day did nothing to erase the evil scenes still tormenting his mind. What kind of depraved person dreams of such malevolence?

Who the hell am I?

MARIE PASSED THE night in a tangle of sheets, tossing and turning, until insomnia finally got the better of her and she shouted, "I give up!"

Startled to wakefulness, Astrid barked. And then kept on barking.

"Shut up!" Marie flipped off the sheets, turned on

every light in the apartment and dressed in her running gear. As she laced up her shoes, her muscles tight, guilt over how she'd treated Astrid ate at her. "Sorry, girl. You know I didn't mean it."

Astrid sat, looking at Marie with round, glistening brown eyes.

"I'm sorry, okay?" Astrid only cocked her head, and Marie felt worse than ever. "Even if some crazy man is on the loose, I shouldn't have yelled at you." She hugged Astrid around the neck. "Wanna go for a run?"

Checking to make sure her phone was fully charged and her pepper spray within easy reach, she trotted downstairs, out the side door and into a beautiful, cool morning. She set out at a record-breaking pace with Astrid loping beside her, and the cloud of fear fogging her mind began to clear.

She formulated a plan.

AN HOUR LATER, fresh from her shower, Marie was recharged and primed for action, while at the same time relaxed. Emotionally, calm. Mentally, focused. Running always had this affect. She went over her plan's checklist in her head.

Step one—George Murphy.

Not expecting a reply, Marie tried calling him one more time, to no avail. But hey, this was the twenty-first century. Cell phones and texts were not the end-all methods of communication. Though direct contact with a field office wasn't allowed, her situation qualified as an emergency. She penned a note to George.

VETSOSDR.MB. George would understand it, and she hoped if he wasn't around, someone else would, too.

She would stop by the grocery store's shipping center on her way to Emma's and send it overnight to the Boise office. It was a risk. But a necessary one.

Step two—Research.

After half an hour online reading every news article or update on Abel Gaines she could find, Marie gave up on learning anything new about him. She spent a few more minutes on amnesia. Seemed retrograde amnesiacs often experienced sharp headaches and limited epileptic seizures. While conditions could resolve in less than twenty-four hours, they could also persist for a lifetime. There were multiple methods of treatment.

Step three—Work on Emma.

It wouldn't solve the actual Abel Gaines issue, but getting Jack out of town would give Marie one less thing to even think about. Although Emma was a softy when it came to hard-luck cases, she was also sensible. If Marie could just convince her that Jack's headaches were clues that he needed serious professional care, hopefully Emma would rescind the offer of a place to stay and a paying job. For his own good, of course.

Step four—Soften Jack up, then convince him to go.

She'd have to just wing it on this step.

"Ready, girl?" Marie grabbed her vet bag, purse and mail and led the way to the SUV. Astrid followed, woofing with excitement.

Driving down the alley behind her building, Marie smiled. "Everything's gonna work out perfectly, Astrid."

In her backseat harness, Astrid fidgeted.

"I'm not being underhanded." Marie looked at her dog in the rearview mirror. "This is self-preservation, plain and simple."

Astrid's tongue lolled out and she panted.

"I know you like Jack, but don't judge me."

Astrid let out a low howl she'd inherited from the beagle side of her ancestry.

A short while after mailing the note, Marie passed under the entrance to the DCA and, despite Astrid's not-so-silent objection, had the plan firmly fixed in her head.

All she had to do now was put it into action.

THOUGH JACK'S FLASHES of memory this morning hadn't included Marie, now he was even more certain they had been acquainted in the past. Just gut instinct. Maybe she feared he might remember something about her, what she was hiding. And she *was* hiding something. Another gut instinct.

After his shower, he dressed and poured a bowl of cereal. While he crunched on milk-soaked granola nuggets, he analyzed what little he knew about himself. His past seemed terrifying. That didn't mean his future had to be. This led him back around to what he was certain about.

I may not know my life's details, but at least I have a sense of who I am now.

He didn't harbor uncontrollable rage. He didn't hate, or hear the call to violence. In fact, what filled every corner of his being was desire.

Marie Beaumont.

A desirable woman, with her deep blue eyes and well-toned curves, what attracted him most was her air of mystery. He had no desire to break down those daunting walls she'd built around herself. Only she could do that. What he wanted was the chance to see what she hid behind them once they were down.

He'd learned over dinner last night that Marie was expected this morning. One of the horses had an abscess in its foot. Jack tugged on his work boots, then headed out.

Maybe today he'd have a chance to find out what the lovely Dr. Beaumont was hiding.

"ELTON, STOP THAT!" Marie blew out an exasperated breath, tucking a loose tendril of hair behind her ear. Planting both fists on her hips, she glared at him. Each time she tried to pick up his foot, the cantankerous horse jerked it from her hand. "You're not going to get the best of me, you stubborn mule."

Elton nickered and swished his tail.

"If you don't like being called a mule, then don't act like one. Now, hold still. I'm trying to help you." She bent down and grabbed the Appaloosa's front foot again.

"Would you like a hand?"

She'd been waiting for him to come into the barn, and still she jumped. Astrid barked and Elton pulled away again, giving her a mocking whinny.

She couldn't stand it when people materialized out

of thin air and scared her out of her wits. She wanted to freeze Jack out, but she remembered *the plan*.

Knowing it was too soon to do a complete about-face, Marie remained aloof. "No, thanks. I've got it."

She tempered her refusal with a frank and hopefully flirty appraisal. *Good lord.* It just wasn't right that a man looked so good in grubby work clothes. And whether she liked him or not, Jack had an impressive set of muscles.

He was checking her out, as well. His head tilted at a jaunty angle, his eyes twinkled with mischief, his grin was wry. Her cheeks flamed and she dropped her gaze. Her plan to soften Jack up sucked. She had no game, whatsoever.

Finally getting ahold of Elton's foot, she set to work cleaning out the sole with a hoof pick so she could check for an abscess. Elton jerked his foot away and tried to lunge against the rope he was tied with in the barn aisle. In the process, he slammed into her, and she fell backward into the wall behind her. Trying to catch herself, she wound up tripping over her own feet and coming down hard on the corner of the muck cart handle with her chest.

Astrid ran to her as Marie struggled into a sitting position on the floor, her breath stuck somewhere between her mouth and her lungs.

Jack was at her side in an instant, squatting so he was eye level with her. "Are you okay? Marie? Say something."

She shook her head. Back and forth, back and forth, her hands fluttering in front of her like hummingbird wings, trying to tell Jack what was wrong. Her lungs burned and her head seemed ready to explode. Tears leaked from her eyes as she struggled to breathe.

"Marie!" Jack grabbed her forearms as she still fought for air. "Calm down—you'll be okay."

Okay? She was dying and he wasn't helping. She tried pulling away.

He took hold of her face, warm palms cupping her cheeks. Earnest gray eyes locked on hers. Their noses practically touched. "Breathe, Marie. It's okay. That's right. It's coming back now, isn't it?"

She nodded, still afraid, then her nostrils flared, and sweet, sweet air flowed down her windpipe. Her lungs expanded, her chest rose. "Ahh, my chest. It hurts." She looked down at her cleavage, where a bruise was already purpling between her breasts.

"We need to take care of that. Can you stand?"

"I don't know." Her voice wobbled; her hands shook. Astrid pushed her muzzle against Marie's arm and whined. "I'm okay, girl. Just need to catch my breath."

"Take a second." Jack took her hands between his and rubbed warmth into them. "Try taking slow, deep breaths."

"It hurts to breathe. But I just hit the edge of that handle there." She pointed at the muck cart, tipped over on the floor now.

"I know, baby, but you need to have that looked at."
He called me baby.

She nodded and he helped her up. "Thank—thank y—"

Marie's legs crumpled like cooked spaghetti. Before she could hit the ground, Jack swung her up in his arms and in that moment, the sting of loneliness hurt far more than her chest. She'd forgotten what it felt like to be held, cared for. Her fingers brushed against his soft, thick hair at the nape of his neck. The unusual light whorls in his stormy gray eyes hypnotized her. How wonderful it would be to wallow in the scent of sun and warm hay from his skin, staying wrapped in his embrace forever.

How's that for softening him up?

What an idiot she was. She hadn't learned one thing since Abel, because if anyone was softening, it was her.

"This is ridiculous. I can walk." One arm wrapped around his neck, the other hand rested against his chest, quite comfortable right where she was.

"All evidence to the contrary." With Astrid following on his heels, Jack carried her to a bench near the barn door but continued holding her, his gaze moving across her face as if memorizing every detail. His mouth parted and Marie touched a finger to his full bottom lip. Soft, especially compared to his perpetual three-day beard.

When he closed his lips around her finger and teased it with his tongue, Marie's insides tightened like a full-body Kegel. She pulled her hand away. "Set me down. I can't leave Elton like this."

Jack placed her on the bench. "Stay. I'll put him back in his stall."

Oh, no, he didn't *just issue an order to me.*

"I appreciate the offer, but he might have an abscess, given the way he reacted with the pick. I've got to check that hoof."

"You sure?"

"Positive. I'm fine."

"Uh-huh." But Jack didn't argue, to her surprise. "Ready to try standing?"

"Ready or not." Marie stood up and stayed up this time. She walked to where Elton was tied. He was still put out about her messing with his foot and tugged his halter a few times to let Marie know. By way of an apology, she rubbed his neck. "I'm sorry I hurt you, but I think we're even, don't you?"

Elton snorted in response.

"I know you don't need any help," Jack said, "but do you *want* some?"

Marie smiled at him and grabbed the pick. "That would be nice. Can you stand by his head and hold on to the halter? Try to keep him quiet?"

Glancing at Jack, she found his intense gaze on her again. But with a smile this time, the effect beguiling her. As he held Elton's halter, his eyes stayed on her as if no one else in the world existed. It was intoxicating.

Get a grip. The plan to soften him up was meant to get rid of him, not become infatuated with him. With the extra pair of hands, Marie finished cleaning Elton's sole. As she suspected, he had an abscess that hadn't yet broken, so she applied a poultice to help it drain.

Although Marie stood straight and tall, her insides softened into mush. How long since she'd had a partner, someone to share the workload, lighten the burden? Someone who carried you when you couldn't walk and cared when you were hurt? She blinked away a burning dampness behind her eyes.

After ten minutes, she removed the poultice. She packed up her vet paraphernalia while Jack led Elton to his stall. "Thanks, Jack. I mean it."

"Any time. And I mean it, too."

Now what?

"Well, I guess I better get going. I've got patient appointments at the office this afternoon."

With Astrid on one side of her and Jack on the other, she walked from the barn into the midmorning warmth of a typical August day, pulling the neckline of her tank top down in a V just enough to see the bruise.

"Maybe you should put a bag of ice on that before you go." He waved his finger in the general direction of her chest. "For the swelling."

She turned to face him while walking backward toward her vehicle. "Nah, it's mostly just a bruise. I'll ice it when I get to the clinic." She waved and spun back around.

"Lucky ice," Jack muttered.

"I heard that," she called over her shoulder.

Driving home, Marie talked to Astrid. About her plan to get rid of Jack, which was failing miserably. About her feelings toward him, which fluctuated often enough to make her dizzy. About Abel Gaines, who was on the lam and had sworn to kill her.

Maybe it was time for her to run, too. Pack some clothes, take Astrid and disappear. She wasn't supposed to, according to WITSEC rules. But according to those same rules, there would always be a case deputy to help her if she was in danger. So much for that. It was time to start playing by her own rules.

Chapter Six

Two young boys chased each other around Marie's legs Friday evening at the Bartwell's fundraising barbecue. "Will you kids please stop pestering this nice lady?" A harried woman jumped up from a picnic table and came after them.

"It's all right." Marie laughed. "They're just blowing off steam."

The woman grabbed each boy by an arm, puffing a loose strand of hair from her face. "Sorry about that. Too much sugar, I'm afraid. Boys, tell the lady you're sorry for bothering her."

"Sorry," the boys said in unison, looking anything but apologetic.

"Not a problem." Wearing a genuine smile, Marie's heart warmed as she watched the young mother direct her rambunctious offspring back to the family's table.

The boys' enthusiasm infected Marie, and an effervescent tingle raced across her body. The owners of Bartwell's had taken full advantage of its location to host these fundraising shindigs. Sawhorse barricades blocked traffic at both ends of the Third Street alley, where the huge warehouse-turned-brewery loomed. They'd filled the space with picnic tables, a play area for the kids, even a portable dance floor where a local bluegrass band had just started playing.

Before coming out tonight, Marie decided to set aside her worries and simply enjoy the revelry. For just one night this week she'd be alert, but relaxed. Free to relish the savory scents of barbecue, the twinkle of colored rope lights and the promise of toe-tapping tunes. And perhaps Jack would show up. Not that she cared, beyond the opportunity to work toward her plan to get rid of him.

That she'd changed into a colorful cotton blouse, shorts and strappy sandals no way implied she was dressed to impress him. Not in the slightest. Appropriate dress for a muggy evening, that was all. Marie ignored the subtle hint of expensive perfume she wore as she mingled with Jasper's townsfolk and exchanged brief pleasantries before moving on.

Get-togethers of this type, she could handle. Casual small talk. No deep conversations or probing questions that forced her to lie. But despite the festive atmosphere and the promise she'd made herself, Marie maintained situational awareness.

She had to, since she'd left Astrid in the apartment tonight. The crowds, loud music and mouthwatering food on the grill would send the poor dog into sensory overload. Last time Marie had brought her canine protector to a party like this, Astrid had eaten something she shouldn't have. It had been touch and go for a few days, and Marie swore she'd never endanger Astrid's life in exchange for her own.

Liz caught Marie's eye and waved at her, then disappeared into Bartwell's with a group of her friends. Although a few different beers were featured on tap outside for the party, anyone wanting a more artisanal brew could slip inside and request it in a plastic cup. Proceeds still went to the benefit. Liz and her book club, which did more drinking than reading, leaned toward the fancier ales.

When a heavy arm encircled Marie's shoulders from behind, she reacted immediately, twisting loose from the hold and spinning toward a man she'd never seen before. Her mind shouted danger, and her body responded accordingly, muscles tightening, fists balling and her flight instinct poised at the ready.

In the next heartbeat, Marie reappraised the threat level. The guy, a tourist by the looks of him, did not have the appearance of one of Abel's men. He leered at her with bloodshot eyes, his gaze traveling the length of her and back, stalling at breast level in both directions. His tongue crept out and circled his lips with moisture before disappearing back into his mouth. Marie's nose crinkled with distaste. Did he honestly think that was sexy?

"Hey, babe. Wanna dance?" Judging by his slurred words, the beer he held wasn't his first of the evening.

Marie's fear diminished until only disgust remained. Not wanting to engage with him at all, she turned and took a step away.

His heavy hand came down on top of one shoulder,

pulling her back toward him. "Come on, babe. Don't do me like that."

Man, did you pick the wrong woman to mess with.

Harnessing every bit of nearly a week's worth of pent-up fear and frustration, Marie rammed her elbow straight back into his solar plexus. His hand fell from her shoulder, and she looked back to see his beer cup hit the ground as he grabbed his lower chest with both hands. His eyes narrowed to slits. "You bi—"

He jerked backward as if by invisible strings, bellowing. Jack, towering over him, jammed an elbow in his back under the shoulder blade, locked his arms and made any movement impossible. The violence of Jack's response happened so fast, it stunned Marie. Sure, she'd hoped to see him here tonight, but not like this. And again, she questioned who Jack really was. Why he'd been found in Jasper. How he knew she had once been a blonde.

"This guy hurt you?" Over the concern in his question, Jack's voice carried a frightening edge of anger.

"No. I took care of it myself." Okay, she sounded like an unappreciative harpy, but it aggravated her to be in a situation where Jack assumed she needed a savior. On the inside, though, in that secret place where she was most vulnerable, Marie was charmed by his gallantry. "But thank you."

Jack frog-marched the guy past Marie, shoved him against the wall of the brewery and kicked his feet into a wider stance.

Jason emerged from the crowd, holding Tashya's

hand. "Whoa, dude. You looking for a job with the JPD? We do have an opening coming up soon."

Jack looked over his shoulder. "Huh?"

"We have a rule around here that the citizens leave the arresting to actual cops." Jason smirked and gave Jack a friendly punch to his arm. "I appreciate you wanting to save the day, but if this guy needs to be booked, I'll take it from here." He swung a questioning gaze to Marie.

"He doesn't." Marie stepped closer. "Unless he's planning to drive. He's drunk." She laid a hand on Jack's forearm. "Let him go. He didn't hurt me."

"He could have," Jack said, firm but with less anger.

"But he didn't." Marie hooked her hand in the crook of his arm and tugged him away. "Come on—let Jason handle him. I'll buy you a beer for being my extraneous protector."

He let her pull him only a couple feet before he stopped. "Extraneous?"

"Yes. It means—"

"I know what it means." He twisted his mouth to the side, his wry sense of humor apparently returning. "It means I'm irrelevant."

Marie chuckled. "Not exactly. In this case, it means I can take care of myself, but I still appreciate your concern."

"Hmph. Well, don't get offended by my concern in the future. Seems I lead with it."

"I'll do my best." Marie smiled to herself. She liked to boast about how self-sufficient she was, but having a US marshal on speed dial put the lie to her claim. And now that George had disappeared, and assuming Jack was on the up-and-up, she wouldn't complain about a little chivalrous concern.

As they strolled in the direction of the outdoor bar, Marie kept hold of his arm, pleased that he didn't pull it away. His skin was warm, and despite the night's heat, she edged closer to his body.

To the right of the platform where the band played, she caught sight of Emma, Piper and Shane. Emma's widened eyes focused on Marie, shifted to Jack, then back to Marie in exaggerated movements. She smiled, mouthed the words "I told you so" and gave Marie a thumbs-up.

Rolling her eyes, Marie returned the gesture, but not with her thumb.

JACK SURVEYED THE alley while they waited in line for beers. "I didn't expect anything this big. The only thing missing is a traveling carnival with rides and game booths."

"Too much of a liability, and it would cut into the profits. Besides, we've got games." Marie pointed past the picnic tables to an area set up for kids. "Cornhole, ring toss, Jenga Giant, even a basketball hoop." She nudged his arm with her shoulder. "What more could you possibly want?"

Jack looked at her, his gaze lingering on the lips he'd wanted to kiss yesterday. Still wanted to kiss, for that matter. "Oh, I can think of a thing or two."

Glancing up and meeting his eyes, Marie blushed. The peachy hue suited her, and her shy smile caused his chest to puff out. *I want to make her smile like that every single day.*

Beers in hand, they watched kids lobbing bean-bags into holes and tossing rings over spikes. A little girl, maybe five years old, started crying when the boys with the basketball wouldn't let her play. Marie set down her cup and went over to comfort the child. When Jack aimed a full-force frown at the boys, they went from derisive laughing to dropping the ball and running away.

Marie helped the girl get into position near the basket.

"I want to be back there." The tiny thing insisted on throwing from where the bigger boys had been standing.

"Okay, we'll stand there." Marie glanced over at Jack, shrugged her shoulders, then moved to the throw line.

After several unsuccessful attempts, Jack came over. "You know, you're not as tall as those boys were."

"So?" The girl pouted. "Doesn't mean I can't play."

"Oh, you can definitely play," Marie said. "But I think he's going to tell you about an advantage you get." She looked up at Jack, her eyes filled with hope.

"Yes, I am." Jack squatted down next to Marie, so he was face level with the child. "When you're at a height disadvantage, you get what's called an assist." He picked the little girl up under the arms and swung her around onto his shoulders.

Marie handed her the ball. "Now, dunk it."

Jack danced his way toward the basket as if avoiding other players on the court. He stopped next to the basket. The girl giggled, raised the ball in both tiny hands and flipped it through the hoop.

"Woo-hoo! Good shot!" Marie danced around like a cheerleader on hot coals.

After a few more dunks, Jack lowered the girl to the ground. "Know where your mommy is?"

"Still eating, I guess." She bounced the ball. "Can we go again?"

"I think we better check on your mom first. She might be looking for you." Marie took the girl's hand and led the way toward the food.

The future hoops star's mother was indeed looking for her daughter and grateful to have her back.

Jack patted his own stomach. "I'm getting hungry, too. You ready for some barbecue?"

"I'm starving." Marie checked out the blackboard menu for food options. "Hamburger, hot dog, smoked brisket—"

"Ladies and gentlemen, we have a winner. I can't remember the last time I had smoked brisket." Jack paused. "Of course, I can't remember my own name, so…"

Marie snickered. "At least you're developing a good attitude about it."

"It is what it is. I just have to believe my memory will come back one of these days." He conferred with Marie on her dinner choices, then ordered two plates of brisket, potato salad and baked beans. "Why don't you save a couple seats at a table? I'll bring the food."

"Um, didn't you say you wouldn't get paid for a while?" She spoke in a low tone that only he could hear.

"Emma gave me an advance. Said she wanted me to have fun tonight."

"Okay, then I'll get us another couple beers and meet you at the table."

Jack watched her bounce away on the balls of her feet, like a barely contained bundle of energy. A few minutes later, plates in hand, he took the bench across from Marie. He would have liked to sit close beside her, but this way he could study her face without contorting to do it. A natural beauty with her brown hair loose, framing her turbulent eyes and sexy-as-all-get-out mouth, staring at her posed no hardship. But he also hoped her face would jog a memory for him. Where he'd seen her before. Something. Anything.

"It's nice that the whole town comes together to help someone like this." He sipped his beer.

Marie nodded. "Anytime someone needs help, we all try to pitch in however we can. Sometimes it's baby things for new parents who've lost their jobs. Sometimes it's paying medical bills for a cancer patient."

"Did you ever know anyone with cancer? Anyone else, I mean?"

"My grandmother. She fought for years." Her voice trembled and she closed her eyes for a moment.

"Were you two close?"

"I guess you could say that."

Talking to Marie was like talking to an iceberg. For every few words voiced above the surface, an entire mountain of unspoken thoughts and secrets stayed hidden underneath.

Jack set his fork down and focused on her eyes, hoping they'd reveal more than her words. "I'm sorry. Did she live here in Jasper?"

Marie popped a potato chip in her mouth, chewing longer than necessary before taking a long, drawn-out drink of beer. "No. She was too ill to travel when I moved here."

"That sucks. Must have been hard, leaving her behind." He piled onions and pickles on top of his brisket and forked a bite into his mouth.

"It *was*. But I had an opportunity, so I took it."

What a sad timbre to her usually melodic voice. *Why won't you talk about your past?* Switching tactics, he asked, "So, where are you from originally?"

She shrugged. "Here and there. Nowhere in particular. What about you? Beginning to remember anything yet? Like maybe where *you're* from?"

He wiped his mouth with a paper napkin, then tilted his head. "A little here and a little there. Nothing in particular."

"Ha-ha. Very funny." She grinned, and it lifted some of the sadness from her eyes.

"You know, it wouldn't kill you to share a little. Like this grandmother of yours. Surely her name isn't a state secret."

Silence. Ten seconds, twenty, forty. What on earth made her so reticent about a mere name?

"I just called her Granny. She raised me."

So, a beloved grandmother fell victim to cancer and

was left behind when Marie moved to Jasper to become a vet. Not that Jasper wasn't a great town with great people, but she could have opened a practice anywhere. Why not stay with her granny? Was it guilt that caused Marie to be so hesitant to open up?

"You must miss her very much."

Marie's eyes filled with unshed tears. "I do." She grabbed a napkin and made a pretense of wiping her mouth but managed to dry her eyes at the same time.

"I'm sure she wanted you to seize that opportunity and be happy."

"She did."

"And are you?"

She rested both arms on the table and met his eyes with an unblinking stare. "Enough about me. What exactly are you remembering?"

Okay, we'll play it your way for now. "It's not like normal remembering. I get flashes of places and scenes. Sometimes when I'm awake, every night when I sleep."

Marie sipped her beer. "Flashes of what?"

It was his turn to hesitate. How much could he share without scaring her? "I haven't wanted to talk about it, because, well, so far very few of the images have been pleasant."

"That sounds ominous. How about telling me a few? You never know, it might help." She leaned forward, elbows on the table, a posture intended to invite confidence. Was she a bit too eager? Did he trust her? Did he have a reason not to, besides once upon a time she might have changed the color of her hair? And realistically, how could he expect her to share if he wasn't also willing?

"I see men fighting, and I hear gunfire. I'm pretty sure someone dies." More than one, but he didn't mention that. He also left out the fire and the blood splattered everywhere. As if his words conjured the very images he desperately wanted to avoid, the pain in his head increased. His stomach roiled. Jack grimaced against the onslaught and closed his eyes to block out the sights.

Marie took hold of his hand. "Is it one of your headaches?"

Her cool fingers acted like a soothing damp cloth laid across his brow. His pain lessened, his stomach settled. "It's passing." Jack opened his eyes.

"Jack, these headaches can't be good for you. It might be a sign of something really wrong. Why don't you go to Boise and have that specialist help you? It's not like there's anything holding you here."

Nothing holding me here. The sting of those words surprised him. To avoid embarrassing himself, Jack looked past her shoulder to where people were milling around the dance floor, waiting for the band to start back up after a break. "Look, I have no intention of going to some specialist in Boise. I wish everyone would just drop it."

Marie's crestfallen face stung him even more than her earlier comment. Staggered by her hold over him, Jack stood and gathered their plates and napkins. "I'm going to dump our trash."

As the band began their warmup, a crowd pushed

toward the dance floor and Jack lost track of Marie. Not wanting to force his way to their table, he wound through the throng, working his way behind the food service counter to loop back around.

As he passed the smoker, the man in charge tossed more cedar chunks in and fanned the flames. The wind shifted. The scent of burning wood hit Jack square in the face, and the images returned with the brutal force of reality. Agony split his brain as if he'd been cleaved in two by a medieval battle axe. He was barely aware of the sweat rolling down his face as he relived the horror. The burning building, red-orange fingers curling into fiery fists that punched out windows, tendrils crawling over sills and blanketing the exterior wall like an ivy of orange flames. The kiss of volcanic heat on the skin of his wrist.

"Jack!" Marie's voice, so distant, broke through his pain-filled stupor but he didn't answer. Couldn't answer. If he opened his mouth he would scream, and he doubted he'd be able to stop. She grabbed his arm and gave a small shake. "Jack. Jack! Are you all right?"

He nodded. Her face shimmered into focus, banishing the heat, the stench, the fear of the fire. Marie's wide, frightened eyes were filled with worry as she tightened her grip on his arm. As before, her touch pushed back the pain. He let her tug him away from the smoking grills and the loud band, down the alley where only a lone dumpster could eavesdrop on them.

Marie dropped her hand. "What happened back there? I had to yell to get your attention."

He took several deep breaths. *Get a grip, Jack.* "The

smoke. It reminded me of a fire. Another of my flashes. This one was just more…intense."

"But you're okay now, right?"

"Besides being a little sweaty, I'm fine." He tried smiling, but Marie didn't appear reassured.

"More intense. Does that mean you remember where or maybe when the real fire happened?"

Jack shook his head. "I have no idea." But he did know two things for sure. One, each headache he suffered was worse than the previous one. A lot worse. And two, Marie's touch eased that pain. Made no sense. Absolutely no medical justification for it. But there it was. Another reason not to go to Boise—as if he was considering it.

They wandered down the alley, and Jack took Marie's hand. "It's nice to be able to talk about this with someone. Other than a doctor, I mean."

"I'm glad I can help, but I worry that your brain injury might be worse than Dr. Saul thought." She paused and turned to face him. "I know you don't want to talk about Boise, but what if you never get your memory back?"

"Would that be so bad? It might even be a good thing."

"You might have family worried sick about you. Parents. A wife. Kids." A bittersweet smile took over her lips. "You were awfully good with that little girl back there. Almost like you're a natural."

Every day since he'd awakened in the hospital, he'd wondered who might be missing him. Parents, if they were alive. His job, if he had a legitimate one. Wife and kids? He didn't feel like he was married with children. But who knew?

He leaned against the wall and pulled Marie against him, pleased when she didn't protest. Like she'd been made for him, she laid her head on his chest and wrapped her arms around his middle. "I can't think any more about my past. Not tonight. It hurts too much. Just hold me a minute. Let me get my bearings."

For several long, wonderful minutes they stood still in each other's embrace. Jack couldn't imagine he'd ever felt so content, and he didn't want the moment to end.

"Jack," she whispered.

"Yes?"

"I can hear your heartbeat. It's slowing." She looked up at him, her mouth parted and inviting. "Does that mean you're feeling better?"

He cupped her cheek with one hand and lowered his mouth to hers. He began with a slow, sweet kiss, not wanting to scare her away. Her lips on his were tentative at first, shy but curious, then grew hungrier. He teased with his tongue. She kissed, licked, nipped his bottom lip. Weaving his fingers in the silky strands of her hair, he eased her head back and tasted her mouth. Spice, hops and something so incredibly alluring.

Pop! Pop! Pop! Bang! Bang! Pop! Pop!

Jack threw Marie to the ground, covering her with his body. Guns. Shooting. Blood. Death. Raging pain in his head. Too much pain. Danger everywhere. More pain.

A group of kids escaped from behind the dumpster,

pointing at Jack and Marie and laughing as they ran back to the crowd.

"Are you all right?" Marie's voice, in his ear.

He lifted his head and looked around. *Alley. Barbecue. Party.* He looked down. *Marie.* Beneath him, looking up at him with wide blue eyes. Her lips, only inches away, tempted him. Hell, the entire length of her body, pressing against his, tempted him.

"What just happened, Jack?" She reached up and took his face in both her hands.

"I thought…gunfire…so real."

"It's okay. It was just some kids with firecrackers."

As her touch soothed away the pain, humiliation overcame him. He rolled off Marie and stood.

Marie sat up. "Better now?" Her words were kind, her eyes concerned.

"Fine." He reached out a hand to help her up.

She laid a hand on his arm. "You don't really seem fine."

"I'm just frustrated. Tired of not remembering anything important about myself. Fed up with dreams and images and reactions to things that make no sense."

"I'm sorry you're having to go through this." She glanced around at the party. "Do you want to go inside, where it's quieter? Get a couple beers and talk?"

He knew Marie was trying to be kind, and he appreciated it. "I'd like nothing more, but I think I should call it a night. I need to…" Jack shrugged.

"Recenter yourself?" Marie still held on to his arm, her touch warming his skin.

"I'd need to know my center before I can do that."

He chuckled. "I just need to get some space, try to understand everything."

"I get it. But if you want to talk…" Her blue eyes sparkled with invitation.

Jack nodded, then cradled her face in his hands and kissed Marie as if she were his salvation. "Thanks." As he walked away, he glanced over his shoulder at her. She stood rooted to the spot, an indecipherable look on her face.

And Marie Beaumont was near the top of his list of things he wanted to understand.

But how?

Chapter Seven

Saturday evening, Marie lounged in her favorite couch potato attire, cuddling a throw pillow while stewing on Jack's behavior at the barbecue. With the benefit of space and time, she realized his reaction mimicked what she knew about PTSD. Clearly, he'd endured some sort of trauma. Something to do with guns and a fire. And it wasn't like she hadn't seen the scar on his wrist, the one that looked like a burn. So, the real question was, did his trauma have anything to do with Abel Gaines, and had Abel sent Jack to deal with her?

Her knee-jerk reaction said no way. He may not know his past—and by now she believed the amnesia was real—but the Jack she was getting acquainted with had to be who he was at his core. And that Jack skewed toward protective, not homicidal. Someone accepting and courteous. The only time he'd exhibited violence was when he thought she was in trouble.

She pointed the remote at the TV and changed the channel to some comedy show. Didn't matter which one, she wasn't paying attention. But the background noise took away some of the loneliness of a Saturday night spent in an oversize pink T-shirt and sloth-covered leggings while eating a pint of coffee ice cream straight from the carton. She dropped the remote on the couch, scooped another spoonful into her mouth and continued thinking about Jack from every angle.

One thing for sure, he was handsome. And he could kiss the starch right out of her knickers. Still, with George Murphy ghosting her, why take a chance by muddying her life with such a complicated man? Under the circumstances, her plan to get rid of him still seemed the safest course. With his headaches worsening, she should keep trying to convince him that Boise was his best option.

Her phone rang. Caller ID read DCA. "Hello?"

"Marie, this is Jack. Amaya's in labor, and I think something's wrong." His words came fast, hinting at panic.

Marie tossed away the throw pillow and sat up. "Okay, slow down. Tell me why you think something is wrong?"

"She's been pacing, seemed to have contractions, but no pups. I don't know. Something told me that isn't normal."

"Okay. Keep her calm. I'm on my way."

Fifteen minutes later, plagued with worry, Marie raced into the kennel with her vet bag in hand and Astrid on her heels.

Amaya was gaining strength, but some birth complications could be too much for her body to handle. After everything the poor dog had endured, Marie refused to lose her now.

"Where are Emma and Tashya?" She opened the stall door and went directly to the mother-to-be, who lay on her side, panting. Astrid trotted in behind Marie, who commanded her to sit. As if sensing she should stay out of the way, Astrid retreated to a corner of the stall and watched.

"They took off midafternoon for McCall. Some wedding-related errands, I think." Jack, sitting cross-legged on the opposite side of Amaya, soothed the dog with a gentle hand. "Tashya checked her temperature yesterday and said everything looked fine. Then right before they left for McCall, she checked her again, predicted she'd give birth sometime today."

Marie kneeled next to Amaya. "There, there, pretty girl. I know it hurts, but soon you'll have a brand-new family who will keep you so busy, you won't have time to remember this pain." After opening her bag, Marie pulled on vinyl gloves and checked the birth canal. "She's definitely dilated. How long has she been in stage one?"

"Um, define stage one." Jack had been avoiding direct eye contact since the moment she arrived.

"When did she stop pacing?" Marie felt along the dog's abdomen.

"A couple of hours ago. Then she started straining. Nothing happened and eventually she lay back down. Later she did it again but strained for a lot longer, and I figured maybe a pup got stuck." He finally met her eyes. "That's when I called you."

A small wooden table near the door held a stack of clean towels cut into twelve-inch squares. Marie rose and brought it over near the dog, then turned the whelping box so Amaya was in a better position for Marie to help her.

"Is she going to be okay?"

Marie looked up at Jack's concerned tone. "We're going to make sure she is." She grabbed some towel squares from the table. "The first pup's breech."

"How can I help?"

Marie gazed across at him, once again caught in the high-beam intensity of his eyes. She blinked, breaking the spell. "I'm not sure you can."

"I may not be a vet, but I'm an extra pair of hands." He got up, walked around to her bag and pulled out a pair of gloves for himself.

Marie ran her hand along the dog's flank. Amaya lifted her head and looked back at her.

"It's okay, girl. This first one's decided to come out bottom first, that's all. You do your part, and I'll help it along."

Using her fingers and the towel, Marie started to pull the tiny puppy from Amaya. With all four legs facing forward, there wasn't much to grab on to. But she continued pulling, slow, steady, and Amaya's contractions kicked in.

By the time Marie held the whole puppy in her hand, clearing his face of liquid and stimulating him to a soft cry, Amaya had gotten up and was straining again. Marie glanced at Jack, again sitting opposite her. With some of the towel squares on his lap, he held both hands out toward Marie, and she handed the puppy to him.

While Jack wrapped him in a dry cloth and warmed

him, Marie felt for the next pup. This one also planned on backing out of its mother, but its hind legs and tail were appearing first. A more normal position than the breech. Keeping a close eye on its progress, Marie sat back and allowed Amaya some time. When the dog flopped onto her side, Jack placed the first puppy near Amaya's face.

Studying Jack, Marie's curiosity finally got the best of her. "How did you know to put him in with his mother right away?"

"I think I had a dog when I was a kid." Jack's gaze drifted up toward the ceiling as if searching for answers. "And I'm pretty sure she had puppies. I kind of remember watching, and my mom explaining what was happening."

The second puppy emerged with no help needed. Amaya grabbed it in her mouth and did the cleaning herself. Marie and Jack both sagged with relief, releasing loud sighs like two deflating birthday balloons.

Amaya licked both of her babies, easing Marie's fear of the first one not being accepted.

"Is that it? Only two puppies?" Jack leaned over the box and examined the tiny, squirming creatures.

"Not by a long shot." Marie shifted so she could stretch her legs out straight in front of her. "But she may take rest breaks between births."

Jack copied her position but propped himself up with his arms out behind him. "So what do we do now?"

"We wait to make sure she has no more complications." She pulled off her gloves and set them next to her vet bag. "Or I can wait. Probably no sense in both of us sitting here." She kept her tone neutral, but she hoped he would stay, too.

"I'm not leaving until this is done." His facial features smoothed out. "It's nice to remember something good. Something that doesn't make my head throb."

"Have you had any other memories like that? Just normal stuff, instead of death and destruction?" Marie checked Amaya again, satisfied that she merely needed to rest.

Jack shook his head. "Maybe death and destruction *are* normal for me."

Astrid crept toward them in an army crawl, like they wouldn't notice her if she approached in tiny increments.

"Astrid? I thought I told you to stay." Marie gave her an admonishing look.

"Actually, you told her to sit." Jack's mouth kicked up at the corners when Marie turned the look on him. "Maybe she wants to help, too."

Astrid eyed Marie, then continued crawling over to Jack, licked his face and tried to climb into his lap. She was too big, so she lay down next to him, her head resting on his thigh. Jack wrapped his arms around her and loved her up.

With downcast eyes, Marie pretended to check on Amaya while she sneaked a look at them. Astrid, normally an excellent judge of character, rolled over for a belly rub. Apparently, Marie was the only one who doubted the man's integrity.

Amaya began straining again, and the next two puppies came out headfirst, one right after the other. Needing no human help with these, the new mama licked them until they were clean and breathing.

The next few hours passed with the dog resting, straining, then birthing a fifth pup.

Vehicle lights shone through the windows, then disappeared. Voices, followed by the slamming of truck doors, drifted from outside.

The kennel door squeaked as it opened, followed by quick footsteps crossing the floor.

"What's wrong?" Tashya came into the stall, her broad smile fading.

"Breech birth with the first pup." Marie looked up at the tech. "Thanks for having the towels ready."

"I hoped they wouldn't be necessary." Tashya came closer and peered in at the puppies. "Are they okay?"

"So far, so good. I'm just sticking around to make sure everything goes well."

"And I'm helping." Jack grinned at Tashya.

Tashya raised her brows at Jack, then at Marie, her mouth curling back into a smile.

"Jack realized Amaya was in distress and called me." Marie folded and unfolded a square of cloth in her lap.

"Uh-huh." Tashya smirked. "Well, I'm back now and can help, if you want to get out of here, Jack."

"Tashya." Emma stood near the stall door. "We need to go over our notes on the centerpieces for the reception." She grabbed Tashya's arm and pulled her from the stall. Tashya's laughter faded away as they closed the kennel door behind them.

"What was that all about?" Jack asked.

"Nothing." Marie's cheeks burned. "Emma likes to tease me about...things." She leaned over Amaya, checking the birth canal again. "Just one more, I think."

She allowed the new mama to rest a while longer, but anxiety over the last pup grew. When the new mama finally stood and began to strain, Marie pulled on a fresh pair of gloves and grabbed a few cloths. The ordeal was a lot for the exhausted dog, and Jack scrambled onto his knees and supported her with a hand under her chest.

"I see the last one." Marie held a cloth beneath the tiny head being pushed out into the world. As Amaya strained and the puppy fell onto the cloth, her heart sank.

"No, no, no." Cleaning away fluids and checking for breath, Marie whispered, "Breathe. Breathe."

But the stillborn pup would never take its first breath. Marie wrapped it in a clean towel, placed it next to the pen, and moved so she could sit cross-legged with her back against the wall. She pulled off her gloves and dropped them on the floor.

Jack came over and sat next to her. "I'm sorry." He set his gloves on top of hers, then put his arm around her shoulders.

"This is ridiculous." She blinked against hot tears. "Death is part of the profession. I never react like this. It's just been a crazy week, and I'm tired and..."

Jack wrapped his other arm around Marie, pulling her against him.

The human contact pushed her over her emotional

edge. With her face against his chest, Jack tightened his hold on her, smoothing her hair and whispering that everything would be all right.

Marie tipped her head back and looked up at Jack. "Thank you for being here tonight."

He brushed the lingering dampness from her cheeks, ran his thumb over her lips. She lost herself in his stormy eyes until he covered her mouth with his. Slow and sensual. Warmth filled her, spreading to every nook and cranny in her body, even those she'd thought long dead.

Astrid crawled onto both of their laps and pushed her muzzle into the middle of the kiss.

"No, Astrid. Get down." Marie pushed at her.

Astrid pulled her brows into that "don't ignore me" expression and whined.

Jack laughed. "She makes a pretty good chaperone."

Marie tousled Astrid's ears. "Too good." She must be losing her mind. Get rid of Jack. Kiss Jack. Fear him. Like him. She had to decide once and for all about him. Emotionally exhausted, Marie gave up on trusting her own judgment. It was time to phone a friend.

And just in case I'm way off base, Dotty will have his number in nothing flat.

Chapter Eight

Jack was surprised when Emma waved him over to the house early Sunday morning. It had to be close to eight, but he'd been up for more than an hour, taking care of the kennel dogs and checking on Amaya and her pups. He'd never appreciated how much work went into caring for and training animals. Well, at least he didn't think he'd appreciated it. This amnesia business was for the birds.

Jack entered the house through the mudroom, toed off his boots, went straight to the sink and scrubbed his hands. "Smells amazing in here," he said to Emma, who he could see through the doorway leading into the kitchen. She hummed while pouring pancake batter on the griddle, and the mouthwatering scent of cooked bacon filled the room.

"Good morning." She greeted him with her signature smile.

Jack dried his hands. "Morning to you. What's up? Didn't think breakfast was for another half hour."

"It's not, but Marie called for you. I told her I would have you call back as soon as I could wrangle you into the house. How you get along without a cell phone is beyond me. Would drive me bonkers."

Jack's mind went on high alert. So Marie had called him, had she? That was something new and different. "Well, when you don't have anyone to call, who needs a phone? Besides, can't afford one."

Emma sighed. "There I go again, being thoughtless. Just ignore me. About the phone thing, that is. Not about Marie calling. Her number is on the pad by the phone."

He walked to the phone, an old-fashioned rotary type, hanging on the wall with a cord that looked two miles long. He picked up the receiver and dialed the number, marveling each time at the *click-click-click* as the dial rotated back to its starting position.

He couldn't stop himself from glancing at Emma, who stared at him with brazen curiosity, then favored him with an all-knowing female grin. Right about then, he wished he wasn't about to have this conversation in so…public a place.

"Marie? This is Jack. Emma said you called." Good. Nice and neutral sounding. So far, he hadn't embarrassed himself.

"Hi, Jack. Thanks for calling me back."

"No problem. What's up?"

"So, um, I wondered, and of course you're in no way obligated, but I wondered, if you're free that is, well, I'd like you to meet someone."

The tiniest breeze could have knocked him over. Not at all what he'd been expecting. "This morning?" He tried to buy himself time to gather his thoughts.

She *tsked.* "I know it's short notice, but yes, this morning. I realize it's just about breakfast time over there, so I was thinking I could pick you up around nine thirty. If you want me to, that is."

The most guarded woman in town wanted him to meet someone. Who? "Sounds great. See you at nine thirty."

"Okay. See you then."

"Looking forward to it."

"Me, too."

Okay, nothing witty or sparkling as conversations went, but since he hadn't known what to expect, he'd take it.

Emma held her peace about the call during their meal and the cleanup afterward, but she couldn't hide her Cheshire grin. And that's when Jack understood what was really going on. Marie was taking him to meet someone who mattered to her, someone to look him over. He was about to be tested.

IF JACK PASSED the Dotty test, then Marie would feel much more comfortable about, well, about things. She'd called Dotty right after she spoke to Jack and told her surrogate grandmother that she'd like to come by for a visit, and if it was okay, she'd like to bring a friend.

"Of course, it's all right. The more the merrier. I surely do hope that by 'a friend,' you mean that two-legged stray of yours. Been hearing some fanciful tales about how handsome he is, and I would love to judge that for myself."

"Well then, you're about to get your chance."

"Yay. You just made my week. Or at least my day."

"Gee, thanks."

"Ah, give an old lady a break, will you? Not many handsome men come around the Hills."

Marie laughed. "We'll see you at ten."

"With bells on, my girl. With bells on."

An hour and a half later, after taking more than a little effort with her appearance, Marie and Astrid pulled up to the DCA. Wearing a cheesy grin, Emma dashed over to the car and poked her head in through Marie's open window. "Hi, Astrid, you big, beautiful girl." Astrid gave a pleased bark from the backseat. To Marie, Emma said, "I'm so glad you're finally going out with someone. It's been way, way, way too long."

"I'm not going out with him. We're just going… we're going to… I'm not going out with him, okay?"

"Ooh, I see. Wink, wink." She gave Marie an exaggerated blink with one eye.

Marie shook her head. "You're impossible."

"Maybe, but that doesn't make me wrong."

Marie flicked her hands in a shooing motion. "Go train a dog or something."

"Gotcha. Need some alone time, eh?"

"Did you hear the part about you being impossible?"

"I did." Emma's silly smile faded a tad. "Listen, go easy on him, okay?"

Startled, Marie asked, "What did he tell you?"

"Relax, oh mistrustful one. He didn't tell me anything. This is me talking to you. All I know is, this is highly unusual Marie Beaumont behavior, and Jack—"

she thumbed behind her back "—hightailed it back to the RV to freshen up, if you get my drift."

"Don't be ridiculous." But secretly, Marie was pleased.

Emma shrugged. "All I'm saying is, you know how he's struggling with the return of his memories and with those terrible headaches of his. I can tell he feels lost a lot of the time, and you've become like an anchor for him. I'm just saying be careful with him. He's more fragile than he looks."

I'm his anchor?

"Hey, are you sure you don't mind staying here next weekend while the rest of us go to Tashya and Jason's wedding?" Emma frowned. "It doesn't seem fair, but you're one of the few people I trust with my animals."

"Of course I don't mind. It would be silly for you to drive back and forth to McCall instead of spending Saturday night at the resort there. I'd love to see them get married, but I know you'll take plenty of pictures."

"Thanks. You're the best." Emma waved and ran back into the house just as Jack came up to the car.

"Subtle as a herd of elephants, isn't she?" He climbed into the passenger seat.

Marie gave a snort of laughter. "*Stampeding* elephants, in Emma's case."

"I stand corrected." Jack chuckled.

The car ride was quiet, but not awkward. At least not for Marie. The peace gave her a chance to shore up her defenses, while at the same time prepare to possibly let them down. Which was all very confusing to her.

Liz was a friend, almost like a mother to her, but

Marie had never taken her to visit Dotty. Nor had she taken Emma. Jack would be the first. He'd gotten under her skin, but he was also an anomaly. In her world, that could spell disaster. Besides her secrets and lies, Marie feared making another mistake where men were concerned. Dotty's opinion of Jack would be her litmus test.

Fifteen minutes later, Marie pulled into the small circle drive in front of the assisted living facility. Jack leaned forward and stared at the sign through the windshield.

"Hemlock Hills? Sounds like something out of a Tim Burton movie."

Marie smiled as she turned off the car engine. "Tell me about it, but you'll be pleased to learn that it's named after the non-poisonous variety of hemlock."

"Didn't know there *was* a non-poisonous variety."

"Few people do, which is why most people refer to it as the Hills." Marie climbed out of the SUV. "Some of the residents joke about it, but it's usually best to let them start that conversation."

"Note to self."

They walked inside the ranch-style home, greeted as usual by the scent of lavender and a friendly welcome from Kim Stanford behind the reception desk.

"Marie. It's good to see you and Astrid back again so soon."

"Thanks. Kim, this is Jack."

"Hi, Jack. Welcome to Hemlock Hills."

"Don't you ever get a day off?" Marie asked.

Kim looked down. "Nope, they've got me chained up back here. You here to see Dotty?"

"Yes, indeed."

"I do work a lot of hours," Kim said as she signed Marie and Astrid in on the guest list. "But then, they don't mind that I use any down time to study for my LSAT."

Jack perked up. "LSAT, huh? When's your test date?"

"In October."

"Do you know what kind of law you want to practice?" he asked, and Marie cocked her head in curiosity.

"I'm not sure I want to practice law in the traditional sense. I'm thinking I want to go into law enforcement. Eventually parlay that into a political career, maybe. Who knows?"

"Well, good luck to you. The LSAT is no cakewalk."

Marie gave him a look that asked how he knew that. He shrugged.

"Jack, what's your last name so I can add it to the guest register?"

"Yeah, about that—"

Marie cut him off. "He doesn't have a last name."

Kim's facial expressions segued from confusion to understanding. "Ooh, so he's *that* Jack."

Jack's brows shot up. It appeared that somehow he knew his way around the LSAT, but he didn't quite understand the nuances of living in a small town where everyone knew who you were, even if they didn't know *you*.

Kim scribbled on the guest list. "I'll just leave it as Jack. Enjoy your visit."

"Thanks."

Marie reached down and stroked Astrid's head, but her eyes stayed plastered on Jack. "Come on—it's this way." She and Astrid led him to the bright, airy family room. The TV was off, and next to the large bay window, the bridge table was as empty as the room. "Between the worship meeting and the special Sunday breakfast selections, the Hills' residents tend to get a later start on the Sabbath."

"I see." Jack looked to his right, then his left, down each respective hallway. "From what I saw on the outside, I was expecting the inside to be dark and depressing." Then adopting an announcer's voice with a faux microphone pressed to his mouth, he added, "Although Hemlock Hills, hemlock in this case being of the non-poisonous variety, might be described as lacking curb appeal, it more than makes up for it with a bright, sunlit inside, affording its residents plush, comfortable seating."

Marie pasted on a smile. His attempt at humor wasn't the best, but he *was* trying. "You might have a future hosting a home reno show on HGTV."

"Ah, but then I'd have to quit my poop patrol job."

"It's tough, making decisions when life throws so many opportunities at you. To your left," she said, although with Astrid already trotting that way, directions weren't needed.

"There are so many doors, and none of them have room numbers. How do you know which one is which?"

Marie stopped and turned to look at one of the doors. "Oh, that. I totally forgot. They're about to do some fresh-up painting, so they removed the door numbers before the painters arrive. Not to worry. I know where I'm going." She continued down the hall to where Astrid sat patiently outside the last room on the right.

"Good to know. You going to give me a clue about who I'm here to meet?"

"Her name is Dotty Hazzard. She's my adopted grandmother, a good friend and an excellent judge of character."

"And I'm here to be judged?"

"You're here to meet the most important person in the world to me."

"I'm honored." Jack meant it. Sharing parts of herself didn't seem to come easily for Marie. Actually, it mostly didn't come at all. That she was willing to share with him was an amazing leap of faith.

Her reaction was not what he'd anticipated. Arm up, hand fisted, about to knock on the unmarked door, she stopped midmotion and snapped her head around. "Are you making fun of me?"

"Seriously?" But she made it clear by her narrowed eyes that she was entirely serious. "Marie, I'm not making fun of you. I really am honored. You don't know a hill of beans about me, and yet you trust me enough to meet—" Darn, he'd already forgotten the adopted grandmother's name. "Um, someone you love. Why wouldn't I be honored?"

For several interminable seconds, Jack waited while she deliberated with herself. Who would have thought the phrase *I'm honored* would set her off? What he wouldn't give for just one minute inside that lovely head of hers, to learn what or who had scarred her so profoundly. She finally inhaled, then exhaled on a slow breath. "Sorry. I guess I'm just not used to people talking like that."

"Like what?"

"About honor."

With no idea what to say in response to that sad state of affairs, Jack opted for a bit of levity. He cocked his head and grinned. "Gee, I didn't think I'd be meeting the family so soon."

"Cute. Real cute." But at least she smiled.

"I hear you two out there, and that's just plain rude. Get in here, Marie, and introduce me to this man you're all—"

Marie pushed the door open. "Dotty, I was just about to knock." She headed for the woman sitting in her easy chair, but Astrid beat her there.

Dotty offered up love to the cherished canine. "Who's a good girl? You be sweet to Sassy Cat, and I'll give you a treat before you go. Yes, I will."

"Sit," Marie said, and Astrid sat, allowing Marie *her* time for affection. Bending down, Marie wrapped her arms around Dotty. "It's good to see you."

"You too, my dear. You know how much I look forward to your visits. Now, introduce me to your friend."

Marie straightened and turned to face him. "Dotty, this is Jack."

"Ma'am," he said, and held his hand out for Dotty to grasp. "It's a pleasure to meet you."

Dotty smiled as she took his hand in both of hers.

"Goodness. You might not know your last name, but I guess manners must be genetic because they seem to come naturally to you. It's certainly a pleasure to meet you. Sit, sit. Take a load off. Not you, Marie. Reach up on the counter and get Astrid her treat."

Jack took a seat on the far side of the small couch that sat at a right angle to Dotty's chair.

Marie reached into a glass jar. "I thought you said Astrid wouldn't get a treat until we left."

Dotty flicked her hand. "Bah! Astrid knows I didn't mean it. Don't you, girl?"

"You're just using bribery so Astrid will love you more than me." Marie handed a couple of biscuits to Dotty and then sat on the couch next to Jack.

"So what if I am? It's not like I have that much time left." She fed Astrid a treat. "You'll have this pretty girl all to yourself after I'm gone."

"Please. You're only seventy-four. You have decades more to live."

"Or I could be dead next week."

"Only the good die young." Marie sat back with a satisfied smile on her face.

"Bah," Dotty said again, leaning forward to speak around Marie. "Isn't she mean? I bet you'll treat me better than she does, won't you, Jack?"

He enjoyed this playful side that Dotty brought out in Marie. He also leaned forward and placed his hand to the side of his mouth and whispered. "Yes, ma'am. I'm bound to treat you better, because Marie over here—" he said as if she couldn't hear him "—can be one cantankerous creature."

"Ha!" Dotty slapped her hand on her thigh. "See, there. Both your dog and your man like me better. What do you have to say about that?"

Marie folded her arms across her chest. "I have absolutely nothing to say to such utter nonsense."

"Hmph." Dotty's slow and appreciative appraisal of Jack would've turned him pink if he'd been a blushing man. Apparently satisfied, she said, "So tell me, Jack, what do you think of my little piece of paradise?"

"I think your room is…far out." The phrase sat unfamiliar on Jack's tongue, but it best described the older woman's style.

Dotty's eyes went round, and she nodded. "It's totally groovy, right?"

Marie snorted.

"Trust me—you kids don't know what you missed during the Summer of Love."

Jack, who had just leaned back, sat forward again. "You were in San Francisco?"

"Of course. I crashed with some friends in an apartment right near Haight-Ashbury. Then in '69, we hitched all the way to New York for Woodstock."

"Really?"

Marie rolled her eyes. "Oh, boy, here we go."

But Jack could tell she didn't mean it. She was enjoying herself, and so was he.

Dotty regaled them for nearly an hour on her adventures during the sixties. "Marie, be a dear and go get us some lemonade."

"Jack, will you come with me? I don't have enough hands."

"Oh, for heaven's sake," Dotty said. "Marie, be a dear and make yourself scarce. I want to have a little talk with Jack."

"Well, I guess that's plain enough." Marie levered herself up from the couch and left them alone.

Dotty relaxed against the back of her chair. "Okay, Jack, I know you have manners, but what else can you tell me about yourself?"

"Not much to tell."

"Don't kid a kidder. I know about your amnesia. What I want you to tell me is, since the accident, what you've learned about the man you are, deep down." She patted her heart. "Where it matters."

"Well, I know I don't like bullies. I seem to have a strong work ethic and a sense of fair play. I believe I have honor and integrity, and I know that truth matters." He paused, then added, "And I like dogs."

As if sensing her species being praised, Astrid leaned her body against his leg.

"That's a fine start. Anything else?"

Jack debated, then just let it all out. "I know Marie is hiding something, and she seems scared all the time. It brings out this urge in me to protect her. I don't know— it's like I have this pull toward her that's more than—"

"Sexual?"

He grinned. "Yeah, that."

"Well, don't stop now. You were on a roll. And if you're worried, I ain't the gossipy type. What you say to me will stay with me."

"All right, then. I can't explain it, but I feel like she lies about things despite being a basically honest person. She has a protective wall around her that I doubt anyone will ever be able to break through."

"Do you want to try?"

"I think I want to see what's behind it, but—"

"You're afraid, too. Of all the things you don't know about yourself."

And the things I do know.

"I am. For one thing, what if I'm married?"

"What does your gut tell you?"

Dotty was the first person who not only asked him about his gut feelings but seemed ready to trust them. "I think not."

"I see no reason not to trust your gut on this. What else bothers you?"

"I get these flashes of memory, and they hint of violence." *And death.*

"And yet here you are, no more violent than I am. Means either you're a profoundly changed man, or you were never violent in the first place. Tell me—what other insights do you have about my girl?"

"I know how much she loves animals. Kids, too, from what I've seen. Seems like she'd make a great mother. She keeps herself apart from everyone, even those she's closest to. I don't understand it. I also know she saved my life and now feels a sort of responsibility for me, even though sometimes she seems scared of me."

"And?"

"And I know I care about her."

"Ah, there it is."

There it was. He cared about her. More than cared.

Dotty allowed him a moment of congenial silence while he wrapped his head around the notion.

"Well, Jack, seems to me you know a lot more about yourself than most folks who have never lost their memories."

"Means a lot to me that you think so."

Banging came from outside the room. "My hands are full. Could someone open the door?"

Jack jumped up and opened it just as Marie was about to kick the door again. He grabbed two of the three cups of lemonade, handed one to Dotty and sipped from the other as he sat down.

"What'd I miss?" Marie reclaimed her place on the couch.

Dotty sipped her lemonade. "Not much, dear. Jack and I were just getting to know each other."

After downing the rest of his lemonade, Jack asked, "Where's the guest restroom?"

"Bah, use mine. It's just through there." She pointed at a partially closed door in her room.

"For heaven's sake, Dotty. Be a dear and tell me where the guest restroom is so Marie can talk about me behind my back." Jack aimed a mischievous smile at the septuagenarian.

"Ah ha ha!" Dotty cackled, slapping her thigh. "You're a hoot. Just go out the door and turn right. You'll see it. It's just down the hall."

"Thanks. I'll be right back."

As he was closing the door, he caught Marie whispering, "What do you think?"

He shut the door without hearing Dotty's reply and

looked down a hallway with several closed, unlabeled doors. Great. He could just imagine walking into someone's room when they least expected it.

Shrugging, he started with the doors at the end. The first one was full of brooms, mops and cleaning supplies. The door next to it was an exit with a keypad requiring a code to open it. The next door coming back toward Dotty's room had oxygen canisters with a large refilling machine along the back wall. He should have started with the door between that room and Dotty's. It revealed the small guest bathroom, which he gladly availed himself of, taking great pains to give Marie time to grill Dotty.

After judging he'd been gone long enough, he returned and knocked on Dotty's door.

"Thought you fell in," the older woman teased.

"Took me a while because none of the doors were marked."

"Shoot, forgot about that. Sorry."

"Not to worry. Found it on the fourth try."

"Good for you. I like a man who doesn't give up when he's going after something he wants." She aimed a quick wink at him. "So, what are your plans for the rest of the day?" Dotty asked them both.

Jack shot a questioning glance at Marie, who shrugged. "I thought maybe we could grab lunch somewhere," he said. "I don't need to be back to DCA until late afternoon."

"Then you should get going before the lunch rush starts. And I have to get ready for my PT." Dotty stood, followed by Marie and Jack. "It was nice meeting you, Jack."

"The pleasure was mine. I hope we can visit again soon."

"Any time you like." Dotty tipped her head toward Marie. "If she won't bring you by, you just come alone. We'll give all these old fogies something to talk about, me with a gentleman caller." She cackled again.

Smiling, Jack nodded. "It's a deal."

Dotty hugged Marie, then waved for Jack to come closer and give up a hug, too. He did, enjoying the maternal-like embrace. With no idea if he even had parents or grandparents still living, Dotty's hug brought him a sense of family.

"Now, you two scoot. Go have some fun." Dotty winked again. "Then come back soon and tell me all about it."

Jack held the door open for Marie and Astrid to precede him. After the door swung shut behind them, he asked, "Did I pass the test?"

"Test? I don't know what you're talking about." Marie's dazzling smile couldn't be much bigger, and her step had a fresh spring in it.

"Fine, play it your way. But I know she liked me. Old ladies like me." A wet snout pushed its way into Jack's hand. "And dogs. Old ladies and dogs like me." He petted Astrid's head.

"I'm assuming you're basing that on your limited experience with Dotty and Astrid, since you couldn't possibly remember that from before." Marie's smile turned smug. "And it's too bad for you I'm not an old lady or a dog."

"You," Jack said, sliding his arm around her waist, "are in a category all your own. And you like me, too."

Marie laughed. "In your dreams."

Marie didn't belong in his dreams. No one good did. His dreams were reserved for evil and malevolence.

But maybe, like his memories, his dreams would get a second chance, as well.

Chapter Nine

A blast of noonday heat greeted them when Marie, Astrid and Jack walked out of the Hills, and she raised her arm to shield her eyes from the sun's glare. On the walk to her car, Marie's elation ran the gamut, from happy to grateful to relieved. She hadn't been sure what to expect, bringing Jack to meet Dotty.

She tapped her key fob and unlocked the RAV4. Bottom line, Jack had absolutely nothing to gain by coming here today, but he had come anyway. In her book, that counted. "Seriously, thanks for meeting Dotty. She did like you. I could tell." The rub was that Marie liked him, too. More and more. That hadn't been part of her original plan.

"I enjoyed meeting her. She's great. Feisty as all get-out and sees a lot more than she lets on."

Amazed that he had sized up her surrogate grandmother so quickly, Marie melted a little more on the inside.

Marie buckled Astrid into the backseat, then Jack held the driver's door open for her and her brows went up. Not something she was used to. Great, just great.

Handsome, muscular, good with animals and the elderly, and also a gentleman. Oh yeah, that plan to get Jack out of town was going up in smoke, all right.

He rounded the hood and climbed in. "You hungry?"

"Starved. What are you in the mood for?" She cranked the engine.

"Anything is fine, only..."

"Only what?" The inside of the car was hot, so Marie turned on the AC.

"Well, I know we just ate at Bartwell's, but when we were there on Saturday, I saw something I think I'd like to try."

"Don't keep me in suspense."

Jack reached around his shoulder and drew the seat belt across his middle, clicked it in place. "Idaho ice cream potato."

Marie laughed. The Idaho dish sounded bizarre, true enough, but she'd defy anyone to take a bite of the tasty creation and claim they weren't hooked. Vanilla ice cream crafted into the shape of a potato, covered in cocoa and topped with whipped cream, made it look like a potato with a dollop of sour cream. "Bartwell's it is."

"But what about Astrid? We can't leave her in the car. It's too hot."

"Ah, just one more great thing about Bartwell's. They're dog friendly."

They entered through the main door, and Marie watched Jack's expression as he checked the place out again. The owners had kept the concrete walls and floors, just as they'd highlighted the high ceilings and exposed pipes and fixtures. Each wall featured at least one large-screen TV, every one of them tuned to either a Sunday sports show or a twenty-four-hour news channel.

"I didn't realize they had pinball machines." Jack pointed toward a corner of the space, beyond the high-top tables and stools.

"And darts, too." Marie indicated a board on the wall. "Some people are begging them to put in pool tables, but I doubt they will."

A young server led them to a table in the back dining area and placed two menus in front of them. "What can I get you folks to drink?"

"You ought to look at the blackboard behind the bar," Marie told Jack as she grabbed her menu. "This place has a lot of great craft beers."

While Jack squinted at the list across the room, Marie smiled at the server. "I'd like your Blood Orange IPA. And a bowl of water for Astrid, please." Marie ordered Astrid to lie down next to her chair.

"And I'll try the Seven Devils Grog."

The server made a note on his pad. "I'll get those for you while you look over our menu." He headed for the bar.

Jack skimmed the menu. "Man oh man. These sandwiches sound good."

"It didn't used to be this way. When they first opened, the food was pretty basic. But when their craft beers developed a cult-like following, tourists started coming to Jasper specifically to visit Bartwell's. So the owners upped their game."

"God bless the tourists." Jack shut his menu.

The server reappeared with their drinks. "Have you decided what you'd like?"

Marie ordered the grilled ham, Gouda and caramelized onions on light rye. Jack settled on the smoked brisket torta with chipotle aioli on a telera roll.

The server picked up the menus. "Make sure to save room for dessert."

Jack and Marie looked at each other and started laughing.

"We forgot about dessert," Jack said.

"The whole reason we came."

They sipped their beers.

"Good." Jack nodded toward his glass.

"Mmm-hmm," Marie replied.

Silence fell. Not exactly uncomfortable, but... expectant. She contemplated which way to take the conversation next. In for a penny, in for a pound. "At the risk of ruining this beautiful day, why did you leave so abruptly Friday night?"

Jack nursed his beer.

"Look, if you don't want to talk about it, tell me to mind my own business. I just hope it wasn't because of me."

"It wasn't." Jack gripped his pint with both hands, holding it tight enough to whiten his knuckles. Whatever he was holding back was hard for him to talk about, and that was something she knew a whole heck of a lot about. "But I *was* upset."

"About what? That jerk who got too friendly with me?"

Jack looked up. "Him? I was at first. I've never liked bullies."

Marie set her beer glass down a bit too hard, sloshing golden brew on the table. "See. That's what Dotty was talking about. You may not know the exact details of your past, but you know who you are. What kind of man you are."

Jack unwrapped his fingers from his glass and pushed it away. "She tell you that? Maybe she has more faith in me than I do."

"I don't think so." Marie took another sip of beer and relaxed against her chair. "Like I told you earlier, she's an excellent judge of character. So, why don't you tell me what happened at the barbecue?"

"I threw you on the ground. I lost it over some stupid firecrackers." The moment the words passed his lips, his shoulders sagged and his broad back rounded into a slump.

Oh, my gosh. It all made sense now. She reached across the table for his hands. He jerked back. She laid hers on the table, palms up. "Give me your hands, Jack."

He didn't move.

"You know what I saw the other night? I saw a man whose first instinct was to protect me. A man willing to take a potential bullet for me." She leaned toward him. "You shielded my body with yours, thinking we were in danger. That makes you a hero in my book."

Jack looked embarrassed, but now for the entirely different reason of high praise.

"Give your hands to me." She slapped her hands on the table for emphasis.

And he did. Large, thick hands, slightly calloused, with blunt clean nails.

"What happened to you was PTSD. Sometime in your past, you suffered something traumatic. That's all. It doesn't make you a bad person, and I don't think any less of you."

He looked at her with that intense gaze that had come to define him in her mind. "What if I didn't suffer trauma? What if I caused it?"

Oh, wow. She certainly hadn't considered that angle. "Think about what you're saying. You're talking about a man who Dotty approves of, who birthed puppies, who extraneously saved me from that jerk." Her mouth twisted into a sideways grin. The same man who somehow made her feel safe, who held her like she mattered, who kissed her until she couldn't think straight. *The man I want to stay in Jasper.*

Jack gave her a smile in return, small, but genuine. His shoulders squared and his back straightened as he once again became a man to be reckoned with. That her words encouraged the transformation made Marie happy.

"Grilled ham and gouda." The server seemed to appear out of nowhere. Their hands separated as he set Marie's plate down, then slid Jack's in front of him. "And the brisket torta for the gentleman. Can I get you anything else?"

They told the server they were fine, and he hurried off to attend other tables as the place filled up with craft beer enthusiasts and sports junkies. For golf fans, the Wyndham Championship in Greensboro, North

Carolina, flickered on one large screen, while on another, local sports jocks offered their take on the coming college football season.

And, of course, no respectable sports bar in Idaho would fail to feature the Steelheads, Boise's hockey team, as the talking heads discussed upcoming exhibition games before the season started. Other screens featured preseason football and trout fishing while two played the news, the commentators discussing some debate raging in the halls of Congress.

Marie lost herself in a mouthful of gooey melted cheese and sweet, caramelized onions. Checking to see if Jack was pleased with his choice, she found him watching her, his lips quirked into a smile.

"What?" She put down her sandwich and dragged a napkin across her mouth, assuming she must be wearing some of her lunch.

"You were kind of dancing in your chair."

Self-conscious about enjoying her food so much, she tried to shrug it off. "This sandwich is *that* good. What about yours?"

He took a bite, then gave her a thumbs-up while making agreeable sounds. "Mm-hmm."

Marie froze with her sandwich halfway to her mouth. Five of the seven flat-screen TVs flashed pictures of Abel Gaines.

"…the fugitive was reportedly spotted near the Utah-Idaho border…"

The rest of the story faded to white noise. Abel. Heading for Idaho. Coming for her. What else could she think? He'd sworn to get even with her, and now, despite her every precaution, he'd found her. But how? George? Was that why he wouldn't answer her calls? Maybe.

Then the bile in her stomach bubbled up, and she watched Jack from the corner of her eye.

"...AUTHORITIES SAY HE is traveling with at least one other person and is considered armed and dangerous. Those with information should report it immediately to the tip line."

Jack's appetite drained away as the announcer continued with Abel's prison escape and then played footage from his criminal past. All too familiar scenes of a wooded area showed on the screens. Black SUVs with flashing lights drove up on the Gaines compound, billows of dust rising in their wake.

It can't be.

Men in FBI jackets crouched behind cars, being fired upon from people inside an old farmhouse. Footage from a helicopter gave a bird's-eye view of the structure, situated in a low-lying area between the rolling hills of West Virginia. Smoke drifted upward, windows exploded and flames licked the wooden siding.

Sweat popped on Jack's brow. His pulse sped up and his stomach dropped. Pain erupted in his head. He knew that place. Those trees. That house. The flames, the heat, the terrible burning pain. When the footage showed a US marshal slapping cuffs on a man, spinning him toward the camera, Jack remembered that face.

Abel Gaines.

Jack's right hand touched the scars on his left wrist and forearm. He could deny the truth all he wanted, but he'd been in that farmhouse. He'd been there with Abel Gaines. Was the fugitive headed this way because of Jack?

The life he'd only just begun to imagine with the gorgeous vet shriveled in the face of what he truly must be. A criminal. A killer. He looked at Marie and found her staring at him with wide, haunted eyes.

Chapter Ten

"Doc, I can't wait a second longer for Raoul to finish up. Watch the desk for me while I dash down the hall, will you, dear?"

"Go, go. I got you covered," Marie said.

"It's the curse of getting older," Liz grumbled as she hurried to the bathroom.

It was late Wednesday afternoon, three days after her Sunday lunch with Jack. The clinic waiting room was empty, the phone quiet, and Marie, glad for the moment to be alone, rested one elbow on the check-in counter and dropped her chin into her open palm. Her other hand reached down to absently tug Astrid's ear.

Since that awful moment at Bartwell's, when she'd learned Abel had been spotted near the border of Idaho, Marie had drawn three conclusions.

The first, Abel was coming to Idaho for only one reason. He was coming for her, as he promised he would. Whatever noxious mix of psychopathic traits comprised Abel Gaines, including lying about every single little thing, when he set his mind on something, he didn't quit. He'd sworn he would kill her, and according to the news, he seemed intent on keeping his word.

Deep down, Marie had known the truth at Bartwell's the moment she heard the news report. The pleasant Sunday lunch turned awkward, the food tasted like ash and she and Jack finished their meal mostly in silence. Relieved beyond measure when he decided against ordering the ice cream potato, Marie couldn't drop him back at the DCA fast enough.

Sunday night she'd tossed and turned like splattering grease on a hot griddle, terrified for her safety. Astrid spent the night pacing and whining. Monday, the newscasts reported that federal, state and local authorities were convening in Boise to set up a dragnet. But Abel was clever, and Marie spent the day anxious, short-tempered and jumping at every sound.

Liz, bless her, had given Marie space, not once questioning her out-of-character behavior, but poor Astrid refused to eat, sensing her human's distress but unable to find the source.

By Tuesday, she'd had enough. Instead of living in fear like some helpless victim, better to look at her problem rationally, like a disinterested third party. When Abel escaped, he could have fled anywhere in the United States, but he chose to head straight for Idaho. No way could that be construed as a coincidence.

Did he know she was in Jasper? Hope for the best but plan for the worst. A bit of Granny Mae's wisdom. Marie needed to plan how she would protect herself based on the assumption that Abel knew exactly where she was.

And that led her to her second conclusion.

She didn't know what happened to Deputy US Marshal George Murphy, why he'd failed to answer her calls or respond to the FedEx SOS message she'd sent. But whatever the reason, Marie was as sure as she could be that George's AWOL status didn't mean he was colluding with Abel Gaines.

While case deputies made a point to keep their private lives to themselves, over the last five years Marie had learned a few things about the man tasked with keeping her safe. For one thing, George was a family man, married with a couple of grown children. In his sixties and nearing retirement, he'd mentioned a few times how much he was looking forward to taking it easy, maybe getting in some rounds of golf and spending time with his grandkids.

Even more compelling, George had lost a friend during the siege at the Gaines compound. Taken with everything else she knew about the man, she couldn't see her way clear to believing George would have helped Abel, either with his escape or by sharing the knowledge of Marie's whereabouts.

At this point, it really didn't matter how Abel knew where she was. He knew. End of story. A small chance remained that he might not know her as Marie Beaumont. But realistically, if he'd had her tracked to Jasper, a false name presented no real obstacle. He already knew she was a veterinarian, and in the town of Jasper, there was only one vet. Not much of a leap.

She ticked off the inferred facts on her fingers. Abel was coming for her. He knew she was in Jasper, and her false name wouldn't slow him down. When he found her, and she had to assume that he very well might, Marie couldn't count on the US Marshals Service to help her.

That led to her third and final conclusion. This one about Jack. The evidence that he was in cahoots with Abel was certainly damning. A stranger, showing up in Jasper right when Abel escaped from prison. The whole "my gut is telling me to stay" thing. The convenience of his amnesia. All highly suspect.

Even once she believed Jack's amnesia was real, the recounting of his memory flashes troubled her just as much. Add in his reaction to the news alert at Bartwell's, and Marie's cynicism seemed justified.

Anyone in her position, and with half a brain, would have mistrusted Jack. When you pushed aside emotion and examined only the facts, things didn't look good on the surface. But after five years of castigating herself for her poor decision-making when it came to men, Marie finally admitted that she had learned a thing or two. A man could paint himself any way he wanted on the outside. Abel had been a grand master. But on the inside, only a true psychopath could hide his reality.

When Marie peeled back the layers of Jack's external complications, underneath were values opposite of Abel Gaines in every way imaginable. Kindness to the less fortunate, a willingness to lend a hand, humility, gratefulness, respect for life and strength without the need to oppress those weaker. Jack could never be Abel's creature.

Despite how it looked, Marie concluded that Jack was a good man, one she was coming to care for. A lot.

"Earth to Dr. Beaumont? Marie! For goodness' sake, where are you?"

Marie snapped upright. "What? What did you say?"

Liz shook her head in a motherly way. "You're a million miles away. What on earth is the matter with you? You've been out of sorts all week. Are you coming down with something?"

"Just got a lot on my mind."

"Well, I'd say it had something to do with that handsome man with no memory, but you don't have the giddy schoolgirl look about you. Are you sure you're not feeling sick?"

"I promise. Thanks for the concern, and sorry I've been cranky. Tell you what—since no one is in the waiting room, how about we close up early?"

Liz grabbed up the office keys. "You don't have to tell me twice." She hustled around the reception desk, locked the front door and flipped the open sign to closed.

Marie arched her back and stretched. "Raoul should be finishing up with Whiskers any minute. Can you think of anything else we need to do?"

Liz began straightening her desk and putting files back in their places. "Barring any emergencies, we're in the clear."

"Good. Think I'll take a hot bath and get to bed early. I'm pooped." Marie straightened a stack of canine dental health care brochures on the counter. "Oh, before I forget. Are there any calls I need to return?"

"No. We're in the clear there, too. But there was this one weird call. Earlier. While you were in the back."

"We really need to get brochure holders for these." Marie picked up another pile of catawampus pamphlets and began straightening them. "Weird how?"

"Well, for one thing, he asked to speak to Megan, not Marie or Dr. Beaumont. When I—"

The brochures flipped from Marie's grasp and sailed everywhere, like a giant game of Fifty-Two Card Pickup. Her skin chilled as if she'd been coated in a glaze of frost. But it didn't stop there. Cold spikes of fear bored their way inside, numbing everything in their path. In another life, when she'd been another person, Megan had been her name. Very few people knew that.

Could it have been George who called? She knew the answer to that before the question fully formed in her head. George never called her except on her cell. Squatting, she began retrieving scattered brochures.

Liz rounded the counter to help clean up the mess from the floor. "Goodness. I'll order holders for these first thing tomorrow. So anyway, I told the guy on the phone that he had the wrong number, that no one named Megan worked here. Then he said he'd mixed up the names, that he meant Marie."

Breathe. In. Out. In. Out. Forcing herself to take a breath, then another, Marie fought for composure. For clarity. For control.

"I don't know why, but I got suspicious when he

said that. Maybe it was the way he said it." Liz looked up at Marie, her brows knitted together in a frown. "I can't explain it. I just got the feeling he was lying, but that's not even the weird part. I gave him my standard line when you're in surgery or not in the office, that you were temporarily unavailable. And I could have sworn he said that was about to become a permanent situation. It sounded sort of threatening if you ask me, but it was hard to tell since he was mumbling. Gave me the creeps, though. You don't have a stalker, do you?"

If you only knew. "Not that I'm aware of," she lied.

Lies, lies and more lies. She hated that part of her secret life more than anything else. *Keep your poker face on, Marie. Think about this rationally.* Prior to her disappearance, she'd gone through weeks of WITSEC preparation where they drilled into her what to do in situations like this. Unfortunately, the first step would be contacting her case deputy, who she still couldn't reach. *Get a grip. Stay calm.* Mentally, she slapped her face, knocking herself into action. She picked up the few remaining brochures.

"Here's the last of them," she said, handing the bundle to Liz. "And I wouldn't worry about the weirdo. Probably just a client, upset that I didn't drop everything to take his call. Did he leave a name, a number? I'll just call him back, straighten things out." She braced herself for the name that had haunted her for five long years.

"I asked, but he hung up on me. Talk about rude. Caller ID showed unknown, so I have no idea who he was."

"Well then, that's that." Marie stood, watching Liz straighten the pamphlets and set them in a neat pile back on the counter. "I guess if he wants to reach me badly enough, he'll call back. You go ahead and punch out. I'll lock the back door when Raoul is done. See you tomorrow."

Liz grabbed her purse and pulled out her car keys. "I have enough time to grab an extra bottle of wine before my book club tonight. We just finished reading this exciting, action-packed romantic suspense called *Resolute Justice* and I can't wait to discuss it. A fairly new author, I think. Oh, what is her name? Something like Marshmallow, Marshland. I really need to remember it so I can buy the next book in her series. Well, good night." She waved as she hurried out the back door.

Fifteen minutes later, Raoul had settled Whiskers in the kennel for the evening and was headed home for some much-needed study time. Marie locked up and flipped off the downstairs lights. "Come on, girl. Let's you and I have a girls' night in."

Astrid's tongue lolled from her expectant, happy-dog smile.

Halfway up to her apartment, Marie paused when the office phone's shrill bell broke the silence. What were the odds? She took another step up, wanting to ignore the call. But like a death knell announcing her own demise, the ring called her back down the stairs.

Hoping whoever it was would give up, Marie shuffled into her office and closed the door. Then locked it, as if the flimsy wood barrier would protect her. Taking a slow, deep breath, she picked up the receiver. "Dr. Beaumont."

"Been a long time, Megan. Oh, wait. It's *Marie* now, isn't it? You should go back to using *Megan*—it suits you so much better." A raspy chuckle came through the line. "Miss me, my sweet?"

Marie's blood ran cold and her hands began to shake, but she'd been preparing herself for this. She would not allow Abel Gaines to detect so much as a hint of fear in her voice. "What do you want?"

"What I've wanted ever since you turned traitor on me." The menacing, thorny tone belied his soft voice.

"Then I guess that will be one more thing you'll fail at." Marie sat in her office chair before her knees could give way, proud that her voice, at least, didn't quiver.

"Grown a spine since we last spoke, I see."

"And I also have a concealed weapons permit." For once, telling a lie felt good.

"My, my. What a turn-on, but tell me, my sweet, ever kill a man?"

"I won't have to. The FBI will have you back in custody long before you reach me."

"Will they? You sure about that?"

"If you have nothing more to say—"

"Oh, but I do. I asked you once to be my wife, a mistake, I realize now. But instead of loving me as I loved you, you betrayed me. And the result of that betrayal was the death of my baby brother, now lying in the cold, hard ground. Seems only fitting that I share my pain with you. Since that old witch grandmother of yours is already moldering under six feet of dirt, and you have no other family, I wracked my brain for a solution."

"I'm hanging up."

"Fine. But don't forget to tell your canine friends hello for me, my sweet. I'll be by soon with a special treat for them. Real soon."

The line went dead.

Chapter Eleven

The instant Abel ended the call, Marie grabbed her keys from the top of her desk and raced to the back of her building where recuperating animals were kept. Only Whiskers was there, Whiskers, and she was fine. Although she'd locked the back door herself after Raoul left, she checked it again. Still locked.

Marie could set the alarm when she left to protect her patients, and she'd keep Astrid by her side to keep the dog out of harm's way. But maybe the creep was threatening her friends and the dogs at the DCA. It was one thing to have her own life threatened. Marie found herself in this predicament because of her own actions. But it's an altogether different thing to have her friends' lives endangered. Emma was innocent, and even worse, she had no idea what might be heading her way.

Marie shivered. *Don't let Abel be there already.*

"Astrid, come."

The Doberman came to her side, ready to heel. Marie unlocked and opened the door with caution. The setting sun still offered plenty of daylight to see

by, and the parking area seemed clear. Marie set the
alarm, closed and locked the door and ran to her vehicle with Astrid next to her.

In record time, Marie buckled Astrid into the RAV4
and then herself. Rolling through stop signs and ex-
ceeding speed limits, she raced for the DCA. "Call
Emma," she said to her hands-free Bluetooth. The
phone rang and rang and rang. She muttered a curse
as it went to voice mail. "Emma, this is Marie. Call me
as soon as you get this."

There may be an escaped homicidal terrorist com-
ing after you. How do I know? Yeah, about that. Not
allowed to say.

She tried Piper, to no avail. No answer from Tashya.
Even Barbara, DCA's administrator, didn't pick up.
Marie tightened her grip on the steering wheel and
tried to control her shaking hands. Erratic breathing,
sweat rolling down her back, she recognized the symptoms of panic.

You're letting him win. Calm down.

Her logical side insisted there was no way Abel had
made it through countless roadblocks set up all over the
state. If he had, then he traveled through the backcountry and over deer trails, a much slower way to move.
He couldn't already be in Jasper. Still...

She turned down the dirt road leading to the DCA,
fishtailing, sending up billowing dark clouds of dust
trailing behind her car like ominous thunderheads. She
scanned the buildings as she drew to a stop and jumped
out of the vehicle. Nothing seemed out of place, and

yet…where was everybody? She unbuckled Astrid. "Come."

She ran to the house first. "Emma!" In through the unlocked back door. Not unusual. Emma rarely locked her doors. The mudroom. Clear. Kitchen, too. "Emma!" Master bed and bath, nothing. No one in the other bedrooms either. The whole house devoid of life. She tore out the front door, Astrid on her heels.

Running for the barn, her panic notched up. Astrid outpaced her and reached the building first. "Search," Marie called to her, and Astrid sprinted inside.

When Marie heard barking, her heart nearly stopped. Reaching the barn, she slowed her pace as she entered, dreading what she might find. Stopping just inside, she bent over, hands on her thighs, and tried to catch her breath. Astrid pounced and nipped with Amaya, who appeared equally pleased to see her playmate.

"Astrid…" Marie panted. "You scared the life out of me. And you," she crouched down and rubbed Amaya's ears. "What are you doing out of the kennel? Why aren't you with your pups?"

Inside their stalls, Elton and Presley turned big brown eyes on her with complete indifference. She pushed upright, and commanded Astrid. "Come." They ran through the barn, out the rear door, and headed for the kennel. Astrid tore ahead of her, and Amaya limped along at a slower pace. Both dogs raced past the RV and disappeared inside the kennel.

Marie reached the RV, pounded on the door. "Jack!" No answer. She opened the door, peered inside. Everything neat and tidy, but no Jack. She stepped down and slammed the door. Her breathing turned rapid and shallow. She couldn't get enough air. Her hands shook and her heart thundered in her chest.

She sprinted to the kennel. Terrified by the silence. No barking. No whining. No human voices.

No, no, no.

Marie reached the door and flung it open.

THE DOOR OF the kennel slammed against the side wall. Jack looked up from scratching Astrid's neck, Emma from scratching Amaya's. The sun's last rays shadowed the figure who had just thrown open the door like a wild woman. He recognized Marie's lean curves. What he didn't recognize was the chaotic look in her eyes and the heavy panting, like she'd just run a six-minute mile.

Astrid took off like a shot, sniffed the ground around Marie, then sat at attention beside her.

"Good grief. What's wrong?" Emma hurried to the entrance where Marie remained standing like a frozen zombie, staring at them both as if seeing something unbelievable. Unbelievably good or unbelievably bad, Jack couldn't decide.

"Um, everybody's okay?" Marie finally rasped.

"Of course, we're okay." Jack straightened from his crouch. "Why wouldn't we be?"

"Nobody answered their phones."

Emma smacked her forehead. "Left mine in the truck. I hate when I do that. Better go get it." As she passed Marie, Emma drew up and gave her the once-over. "You're soaked in sweat. How far did you run?

This is more than me not answering my phone. Tell me this instant what's going on."

Jack watched Marie transform before his eyes. One moment an out-of-control whirlwind, the next a shuttered woman who seemed to be searching for a way to cover her uncharacteristic display of emotion.

Ever since Bartwell's, when he'd caught the news report about Abel Gaines and then turned to see Marie's surprising reaction to the same story, Jack was certain about two things.

He and Abel Gaines were connected.

Abel Gaines and Marie were connected.

And now, Gaines was on the loose. In Idaho, if you believed the TV. Heck of a time for Jack to be missing his memories.

"Um, I thought something was wrong. I came to make sure everyone was all right."

Jack walked closer to her, stopping alongside Emma. "Why would you think we were in trouble?"

She met his eyes, and reflected in those twin blue pools was unadulterated fear. Her secretive nature had made him wonder, but now he was positive that whatever secrets she held, they terrified her.

"Clearly it was nothing." She turned to go.

"Oh, no you don't." Emma reached out and grabbed Marie by the arm. "You're not leaving without telling me what made you think something was wrong out here. So much so that you raced here to save us. Thanks for that, by the way."

As was her habit, Marie rested one hand on Astrid's head. The other was down at her side, fingers rubbing back and forth, back and forth, small movements not meant to be noticed. Jack noticed. Her face bore a closed expression; her eyes shifted to focus on the ground. Marie was about to lie.

"I got a prank phone call. It worried me, so I came by to make sure everyone was all right."

Emma raised her arms as if talking to the heavens. "What a terrible thing to do. I wonder who it was. I'd like to wring their neck."

In Jack's opinion, Emma was asking the wrong questions. "Marie." He kept his voice soft. "What did they say that worried you?"

"It doesn't matter. Astrid, come." She was shutting him out as surely as if she'd slammed down the gate of an impenetrable fortress, and for some reason that infuriated him.

He raised his voice a notch. "It does matter. What did they say?"

Emma stopped ranting and returned her gaze to Marie.

Marie looked miserable. "I already feel like a fool. Why can't you just drop it?"

"Because we have to report it," Emma said. "Jason is due here soon. We'll wait for him and then report it. Who knows—he might catch the little miscreant."

"I'm not waiting and I'm not reporting it. I'm telling you it was no big deal, so I'd appreciate it if both of you could stop making it one."

Jack frowned. Since day one, she'd been probing and prodding, poking at his memories like a young boy with a stick poked at a dead animal discovered on the side of the road. He had no intention of letting her off so easily. Turnabout was fair play.

"So you received a prank phone call that scared you so much that you raced here and ran helter-skelter to find out if we were okay, but for some reason you don't think what the prank caller actually said is important enough to share with us. Or to report to Jason. And don't bother telling me it's no big deal, because your actions clearly say otherwise."

Marie pulled her shoulders back, and Jack could practically see her adding another two feet to her already high protective wall. What on earth could have happened to her to make her so fearful of opening up? Could it have something to do with Abel Gaines?

"I need some air." She stepped outside, Astrid glued to her side. Like Jack, the dog sensed something not right with her mistress. Also like him, Astrid was in the dark as to what that something was.

Amaya and Emma followed Marie outside. "That doesn't look good." Emma pointed with one hand, shielding her eyes from the setting sun with the other.

Marie followed her gaze toward town, where a thick, vertical stream of black smoke reached into the sky. "Oh, my gosh, no! Come, Astrid." She and Astrid dashed for her car.

"Go," Emma said to Jack. "Whatever is going on, she's in no condition to drive."

Overwhelmed by the need to protect Marie, Jack raced after her.

Chapter Twelve

Tell your canine friends hello for me, my sweet.

"Not the clinic!" None of Marie's "canine friends" were there, but Abel wouldn't know that. And Whiskers *was* there. She couldn't leave the poor cat to burn alive.

Jack beat her to the car and blocked her way to the driver's side door. "Give me your keys. I'll drive."

"Get out of my way!" She squared off with him. "You don't have a license. You can't legally drive."

He held out his hand. "And if you get behind the wheel like this, you'll most likely kill yourself. Astrid, too. Along with innocent—"

"*Fine.*" Speed mattered now, and she *was* shaky as all get-out. She threw him the keys, dashed around to the passenger side, buckled Astrid in the backseat and then hopped in the front. Jack was already strapped in with the car started. He gunned it the second she slammed the door and reached for her seat belt. They raced toward Jasper.

Without taking his eyes from the road, Jack said, "Are you going to tell what's going on, or do you plan to let me walk into something blind?"

"What are you talking about? Nothing's going on. There's a fire. I'm going to help. That's it."

For the second time in as many minutes, Jack raised his voice. "So all of a sudden you're a trained firefighter. Gee, where's your Dalmatian?"

She flashed an angry glare his way, but his eyes faced forward. Well, he wasn't the only one who could shout. "What's your problem?"

"You're my problem. You are—"

"I didn't ask you to come. That was your choice, so get off my case."

"You're lying to me. You've been lying to me since the day we met. Tell me what has you so scared."

"Look out!"

Jack jerked the steering wheel, swerving to avoid a jackrabbit crossing the road. Tires squealed on the pavement, and a hint of burning rubber wafted in through the open window. Quickly righting the car, Jack continued down the road.

"Your driving is what's scaring me."

"Whatever. Can you tell where the fire's coming from?"

Marie snapped to. Instead of fighting with Jack, she should have been paying attention. As they approached the city limits, she could tell the smoke wasn't in the right place for the clinic. Her heart stopped.

"Oh, no, no, no. Jack, hurry. It looks like the smoke is coming from Hemlock Hills."

They drove up on a scene of frightening pandemonium. Two fire trucks, lights flashing. Firefighters held hoses from which white arcs of water attacked a blaze out of control. The entire structure was engulfed. The fire captain's car, two police cars and an ambulance scattered around the perimeter like blinking Legos. First responders everywhere, some running, some shouting, some helping soot-covered residents away from the danger.

"Where's Dotty? I can't see her anywhere."

"Marie, don't panic. You can't go over there," Jack said with maddening calmness, pointing with one finger to the scene of the fire. "They won't let you. Dotty is probably already out. Look, they're taking residents over to the lawn of that house. Let's ask about her over there."

Marie feared this fire was no accident. If Abel proved to be the arsonist, then he would have known about Dotty and would have targeted her. Dotty's room was on the far side of the building where the fire seemed the worst. "Stop the car! Let me out!"

"No. It's not safe."

Spaced between the emergency vehicles, parked cars lined the street leading up to the Hills, and clustered in bundles, gaping pedestrians stood watching the melee. Jack slowed to a crawl and Marie didn't wait for him to stop. She leaped from the slow-moving RAV4.

"Marie, no!"

But her fear for Dotty's safety was so intense, she didn't even unbuckle Astrid. She sprinted for the building.

When they saw her coming, Jasper PD Lieutenants Cal Hoover and Margaret Avery spread their arms. "Dr. Beaumont, stop. We can't let you through."

Fear and panic exploded into a scream. "Dotty's in there! I have to find her!"

"Doc, calm down. You can look for her over at Jim Nance's house. They've set up a staging area and triage on his front—"

If one more person tells me to calm down... She backed up as if in compliance with the officers, but she instinctively knew Dotty wasn't on Jim Nance's front lawn. When Hoover and Avery let down their guard just enough, Marie darted left, flanking them.

"Doc!"

She ignored them, and they didn't follow her. They had to man their post. She tore around the side of the building and pulled up short. Three firemen on a hose blocked her path. Even if they hadn't been there, Marie could go no farther.

The rear of the house was an inferno, scalding heat sending her backward. She gasped for air stolen by the raging fire. What little she managed to find seared her throat. She fell back more.

This was no pleasant hearth fire crackling in the winter. This fire roared at the top of its lungs. And mixed in with the roar were pops and snaps, like bones breaking. The left half of the building collapsed. A shower of orange sparks flickered up into the rising dark smoke like lightning bugs in a midnight sky.

Marie fell to her knees, her hands covering her mouth. She shook her head and wept. *This is all my fault. Oh, Dotty, I'm so sorry.*

Another team of firefighters raced over and brought a second hose to join the effort. Ignored by the first responders, Marie watched the black smoke war with boiling-hot white steam as water began conquering fire. As the flames died, Chief of Police Doug Walters, Lieutenant Avery and Fire Chief Rich Newcomb stood nearby in a huddle, oblivious to Marie's presence.

"We've had one too many fires lately for my liking," Chief Walters said.

Newcomb nodded. "We have, indeed. But what we have here is a heck of lot different than forest fires in the hills."

"Agreed." Chief Walters turned to Lieutenant Avery. "We get everybody out?"

"It wasn't easy to double-check, with no numbers on any of the room doors." She gave a nod in the direction of the makeshift triage area. "Haven't gotten the official head count yet, but the Hills' director just showed up and Cal's working on it. Should have the count to you in a few minutes."

"Good." Walters turned to his counterpart in the Jasper fire department. "Your guys sure about the body?"

Chief Newcomb nodded. "Hundred percent sure. Near the site of the explosion."

Body? Explosion? What little hope Marie held vanished on a puff of smoke.

"Any chance this was an accident?" Walters asked.

"Sure, but only a slim chance."

Avery folded her arms across her chest. "Why's that?"

"Even accounting for the explosion of the oxygen tanks, the fire damage was extensive and quick, suggesting the use of an accelerant."

Marie gasped. The oxygen tanks exploded. The oxygen tanks that were stored near Dotty's room. And... there was...there was a body. A harsh sob escaped.

Chief Walters turned at the sound. "Son of a... Avery, get her out of here."

Lieutenant Avery bent down and wrapped her arm around Marie's shaking shoulders. "Come on, Marie. We have to get you out of this area. It isn't safe."

Dotty's death had been her fault, and defeated by her guilt, Marie simply didn't have it in her to move.

"You know somebody who lives here?" Avery asked, gripping Marie's shoulders tighter.

Unable to speak, Marie nodded.

"I'm going to help you up and take you to the triage area. Dollars to donuts we'll find your friend there."

"But, but the body?"

"No way to know who it is until the autopsy, but odds say we'll find...what's your friend's name?"

"Dotty."

"Odds say we'll find Dotty over at Jim Nance's place. You ready to try standing?"

Marie nodded again and got to her feet, swaying a little. True to her word, Avery kept her arm around Marie and led her away from the smoldering wreck that had been Dotty's home.

They rounded a corner.

"There are a couple of people over there who look like they're waving you down." The lieutenant pointed toward the crowded front yard of Nance's house.

Marie's gaze followed Avery's hand and she couldn't believe her eyes. Dotty, wearing her shiny gold sneakers, her face filthy with soot, held a bundle of singed fur in her lap. She sat in a lawn chair, waving one arm in the air like an inflatable tube man in front of a car dealership. Jack stood at her side, his large hand resting possessively on Dotty's shoulder, his intense look melting Marie's heart even from this distance. Astrid sat in front of them, as if on guard.

"Oh, my gosh." Marie waved back.

"Go," Avery said.

Marie didn't need to be told twice. Still a bit wobbly, she started off at a slow pace but picked up speed. When she reached the chair, she dropped to her knees next to the precious woman sitting there and threw her arms around Dotty.

Sassy Cat gave a low growl but endured Marie's trespass.

"I thought… I thought… I can't believe you're all right." She wiped at the tear tracks running down her cheeks.

"Hush, now. Everything's fine. I'm a bit shaken up is all. Not even a broken nail." She ran her fingers through Marie's hair, soothing her.

"I don't know what I'd do if anything happened to you."

Dotty laid her gentle hand on Marie's damp cheek. "I'm perfectly fine, and thanks to Jack, so is Sassy Cat."

"I really didn't do anything. A firefighter was leading Dotty away from the backyard, and the cat was fighting to get away from her. I just took the cat and brought them both over here."

"Oh, fiddlesticks. This is my rescue story, and I'll tell it how I want to." Dotty whispered to Marie, "He saved us both. He *carried* us over here."

Marie looked up at him, still standing at Dotty's side like her sworn protector. "Thank you," she mouthed, afraid that if she spoke her gratitude aloud, she'd disintegrate into a sobbing mess again.

For the next two hours, while the firefighters made sure the fire was fully out and then began their investigation, the police finally got an official head count, finding all the residents and staff of Hemlock Hills accounted for.

Night fell, almost unnoticed as the sparks dancing in dark smoke segued to a black sky filled with stars. The Hills' director had already made phone calls, ensuring his residents would be well taken care of. Marie and Jack helped see Dotty and the others settled in temporary quarters at the Salmon River Motel.

Since it was an open investigation, no one mentioned the charred remains, but Marie dared to hope it had been Abel, killed in the act of his own mischief.

If it wasn't him, who that Marie cared about might be next on the evildoer's hit list?

WHILE DRIVING BACK to the DCA, Jack glanced at Marie. She was disheveled, smudged with soot and zombie-like. *Not good.*

His eyes went back to the road. He recognized the symptoms of shock, and it worried him. Luckily, she kept a poncho in the car, which he'd wrapped around her for warmth. He'd stopped at the convenience store for electrolyte water and protein sticks, but she sipped and nibbled only when he prompted her.

This was not the stubborn, fiercely independent Marie he knew. Once they'd seen Dotty settled, she had agreed without protest when he'd insisted on driving. More telling, she'd forgotten to buckle Astrid into the car. Now she sat in the passenger seat without talking, pale, knots of tension in her shoulders and upper arms, her jaw clenched.

The prank phone call, the rush to the DCA followed by the rush to the Hills, then the horror of thinking Dotty was dead, had wiped her out. Coupled with the drop in adrenaline, she could barely keep her eyes open. He pulled up to the RV, knowing he couldn't let her drive home until her blood started flowing again. Until the life came back into her eyes.

He unbuckled Astrid, then opened the RV door. But instead of going inside, the dog stayed in the backseat, unwilling to leave Marie. Jack opened her car door, reached over and undid her seat belt. Sighing as if the weight of the world was on her shoulders, Marie swung her legs out and stood, rousing from her stupor.

Jack steered her up the steps and into the RV. Astrid bounded after them, sitting next to Marie's feet when she dropped onto the small couch. After he closed the door, Jack retrieved the bottle of whiskey that Shane had left in the RV as a gift. He poured a small amount into two glasses, then handed one to Marie and sat next to her, their legs almost touching.

She held it in both hands, looking at nothing with a thousand-yard stare. A few minutes later she blinked, her head jerking back slightly, and glanced around. "Where am I?"

"Shane's RV, where I'm staying."

Marie nodded. Noticing the glass in her hands, she took a sip, then set it in the armrest's cup holder. "If I'd lost Dotty…" Tears welled in her eyes.

"You didn't lose her. She's fine."

"But if she'd been hurt in that fire, I'd… I'd…oh, Jack." Marie leaned her head on his shoulder and wrapped her arms around him, clinging to him. At last the tears came, heart-wrenching and agonizing. Jack held Marie as her pain tore at his gut.

After crying herself out, she lifted her head and looked at him with wide, sad eyes. She touched her lips to his as her tear-spiked lashes began to lower.

Jack's heart raced, and every muscle in his body went taut. He shifted on the couch, pulling her against him. Her breathing was quick and shallow; her breasts pressed into his chest. Again and again, every time she breathed.

Through his thin T-shirt, he felt her hard nipples pushing against him, and he went hard himself.

She gasped, licked her lips. "Jack," she whispered.

And there was the permission he needed. Passion broke the dam of his restraint, and he crushed his mouth to hers. She opened to him immediately, her tongue sparring with his. Panting like he'd climbed a mountain, he couldn't seem to catch his breath. Suffocating never felt so sweet.

They stood while she tugged frantically at his shirt, and he hurried to help her remove it. He pulled hers off and began guiding them to the back of the RV, their mouths never breaking contact. Moving as one, they bumped into the kitchen counter, got held up by the bathroom door. Jack slammed it closed and propelled them into the bedroom.

They fell on the bed as one, facing each other, kissing each other. He fumbled with her bra strap. When he finally removed it and held her bare breasts in his hands, Marie moaned. Warm, soft mounds, capped by pinnacles of desire. He thumbed the twin peaks, and she arched against his palms.

He rolled her onto her back, unfastened her jeans and slid them down her legs. Standing, he stared down at her from the foot of the bed, fumbling with his fly.

Marie, naked and waiting for him with greedy eyes…nothing had ever looked so enticing. He ached from wanting her. Apparently impatient herself, she sat up and moved to the edge of the bed. As soon as his jeans hit the floor, Marie slid her warm fingers beneath the waistband of his boxer briefs. She didn't take the time to tease him with her hands or mouth. Instead, she tugged his shorts down past his knees. They dropped the rest of the way and he stepped out of them.

Biting her bottom lip, Marie looked at him with a longing that nearly undid him. He lowered himself on top of her, and they resumed their kissing.

They rolled across the sheets, stopping with her on top, Jack loving the weight of her. They rolled again, this time with him on top. Her legs fell open to cradle him and he pressed himself against her slick opening, using every drop of willpower to hold back from entering.

She groaned, thrashing beneath him, her hands latching on to his buttocks, pulling him closer.

"Marie," he groaned. "Protection."

"I've got it covered. Jack...please."

No force on earth could have stopped him then. He thrust inside her and the world tilted on its axis. She tightened around him. Hot. Wet.

Marie gasped and bucked. "Harder."

He levered himself up on his arms and did her bidding. Taking her, possessing her, giving her all of him in return.

Fisting the sheets in each hand, Marie arched again and cried out, her muscles taut, her body quivering. Jack plunged deep within her, groaning with pleasure as Marie tightened and squeezed, again and again. He finally could wait no longer and shouted his own release.

He collapsed on top of her, each of them struggling to catch their breath, their bodies slick with sweat, desire pooling where they were joined. Though loath to separate, he rolled off her, spent and fulfilled at the same time. She cuddled into his side, and he brushed a tendril of hair away before kissing her forehead. They lay like that until their heat dissipated and Marie shivered.

"You okay?" His voice came out raspy.

"Mm-hmm," she murmured. "Except, I'm thirsty."

"Water or whiskey?"

"Whiskey, I think."

He got up, walked naked to the other room and grabbed their glasses and the bottle. When he returned to bed, he found she'd wiggled under the sheet and propped herself up against the pillows, watching him with eyes that still sparkled with desire.

He got in bed beside her, topped off each glass and handed one to her.

She took a sip. "You know what I was thinking?"

"I'm surprised you can think at all. More than I'm capable of." He sipped from his glass, enjoying the liquid heat burning down his throat and into his stomach. "So tell me, what were you thinking?"

She set her glass on the bedside table. "I was thinking that if you and I, here, like this—" she spun her index finger around to encompass the bed and the two of them in it "—had been a scene in an old movie, we'd be smoking cigarettes right now."

He stared at her, not comprehending.

"You know, like they used to do after a particularly steamy sex scene. Of course, we don't, but if we smoked, what we just did would definitely be cigarette-after-sex worthy."

Jack laughed.

She smiled. "What?" Then she started laughing, too, and punched his arm. "Stop laughing at me."

He responded by doing an exaggerated parody of smoking, which made them both laugh harder.

It took a while, but eventually the laughter slowed to hiccupping chuckles, finally leaving them both silent and smiling.

He pulled her into his embrace and kissed her

whiskey-glazed lips. Taking his time this go-round, Jack replaced the frantic groping and desperate need with gentle exploration. Skimming his fingers across her satiny skin, learning her peaks and valleys, making note of what pleased her, was not something to be rushed.

His fingers sought her center, where he massaged, rubbed and probed until she shook with climax after climax. Only then did he enter her. Only then did he seek his own release. They chased each other to unknown heights, peaking together, then drifting back to earth in each other's arms.

Sitting back against the pillows, processing what had just passed between them, they turned to each other as if on cue and puffed on invisible cigarettes, smiling at the type of private joke only lovers shared.

"Come over here." Jack moved so that Marie could nestle against his side. "How did Dotty come to be your adopted grandmother?"

She held her glass before her lips, and he thought she was about to clam up on him.

"Sassy Cat," she said, and told him about her house call on behalf of the residents' adopted feline.

Pleased Marie was sharing, Jack kept his mouth shut and enjoyed her story. The longer she spoke, the more animated she became. When she paused for another sip, he asked about her real grandmother.

"Oh, Granny Mae was the best. I wish you could have met her. She put her life on hold to raise me. And then, when it should have been her time to travel or do whatever she wanted, she was diagnosed with cancer." Marie raised her eyes to meet Jack's. "Life can be so unfair."

"I didn't mean to make you sad."

"You didn't. I'm glad you asked. I don't get many chances to talk about her."

And she chose me to listen. A warmth spread throughout his chest that had nothing to do with the whiskey. "Want to do something fun this weekend? Just you and me?"

Yawning, Marie asked, "Like what?"

"White water rafting."

"As long as we don't go down any hard ones. I'm not very good at it."

"But you'll go?"

"I'll go if you let me sleep now."

He kissed the top of her head, gratified that she was staying the night, that he would wake with her beside him.

They slid down in the bed, Marie snuggling next to him. As exhaustion overtook him, he marveled at the turn his life had taken. And yet, insidious seeds of doubt ate at the edges of his newfound joy. Dreading the specter of his unsavory past that was sure to visit him in his dreams, Jack focused on their night of lovemaking. But even as he did, an uncomfortable question pecked at his brain.

Why does something so good feel so wrong?

Chapter Thirteen

Early the next morning Marie left a note for Jack, and she and Astrid slipped out of the RV without waking him. He deserved his rest after last night. A grin took over her mouth and her cheeks flushed with warmth.

She glanced in the rearview mirror, coming eye-to-eye with Astrid. "Oh hush. It's not like I do this all the time." *But last night with Jack definitely made up for the long dry spell.*

Astrid huffed.

Marie parked outside her office, and she and Astrid dashed up the outside stairs to her apartment. After a quick shower and change of clothes, she fed Astrid and asked Liz by text to please walk the dog when she got to the office.

Then she locked up and walked toward Millard's Diner, intent on unearthing information about the Hemlock Hills fire.

The diner's policy was to sit wherever you wanted, so when Marie entered, she grabbed an empty booth near the front.

Vera Millard stopped at the table with an empty mug and a full carafe of coffee. "You need a menu?"

"No thanks. Just coffee." Marie smiled up at her.

"Something happen to Liz?" Vera set down the mug and filled it. "She always picks up your coffee, doesn't she?"

Shaking her head, Marie said, "No, Liz is fine. I just felt like popping in this morning."

"Hmph." Well-known for her cantankerous demeanor, Mrs. Millard seemed to be in true form today.

After Vera moved on with her carafe, Marie relaxed against the vinyl back of her bench seat, nursing a cup of coffee and biding her time. When the diner's door swung in, its chime announcing another arrival, Marie looked up. *Finally.*

Officer Ava Callan joined three other JPD officers sitting at the blue Formica counter. Marie was better acquainted with Ava than the other cops who'd come in so far. This would be her chance.

"Ava." Marie raised her voice to be heard over the din of the other diners.

Ava turned and Marie waved her over. The policewoman said something to the cop next to her, grabbed her coffee and joined Marie.

"This is a nice surprise. I thought Liz picked up your coffee on her way in." Ava slid into the booth.

"Good grief. Does everyone know my habits and schedule?"

Ava chuckled. "Small towns. After living in Chicago, the hardest thing to get used to here is having everyone all up in your business." She shrugged. "But you've been here longer than me. It gets easier, right?"

"Ask me in another ten years. I might know by then." But chances were, in ten years Marie would still be walking the tightrope between loneliness and safety. The main reason she didn't frequent Millard's was the same reason she didn't date or join a book club or go dancing. The less she hung out in the same places with the same people, the fewer probing questions about her past she had to fend off. She'd already learned that once you got past the small talk, once you forged a bond with a group of people and once that group started baring their souls to you, they expected you to reciprocate.

And that could never happen. The only reason Marie was in Millard's now was to find out what she could about the fire and the burned body. She should have come up with a better plan, since apparently her appearance in the diner was headline news.

She gave Ava a warm smile. "How's Lacey doing?" Marie had operated on Ava's K-9 partner a couple months earlier, after the dog was injured in a bomb explosion.

"Great. After her last follow-up with you, I started easing her back into her duties. She's good as new now."

"Glad to hear that. Thank goodness she wasn't burned in the explosion." Marie cringed internally at her awkward segue to yesterday's incident.

"That would have been horrible." Ava stirred sugar into her coffee. "Speaking of fires, I saw you at Hemlock Hills yesterday, didn't I? And who was that fine man you brought with you?"

But the segue worked.

"I saw the smoke and wanted to make sure everyone was safe." Marie shook her head. "I can't believe Dotty managed to save that darn Sassy Cat and still get out unscathed."

Ava arched a brow. "And the fine man?"

"That would be Jack. Astrid and I found him injured outside of town a couple of weeks ago."

"That's the guy with amnesia? Dang, girl. When you're out finding strays, you don't mess around." Ava gave her a sly grin. "You two an item already?"

With her cheeks warming, Marie scoffed. "Hardly. We barely know each other." She took a sip of coffee. "But we're going rafting this weekend."

"That should be fun."

"I hope so. I've only gone a few times, so I want to make sure we stay on the easier rapids."

"Maybe you can just fall over the side and let him rescue you." Ava pretended to swoon in the booth, fanning herself with one hand.

Marie shook her head. "My two main goals are to not look stupid and not drown. Maybe not in that order." She waited for Ava to stop laughing, then switched back to their original topic. "So have they figured out what started the fire? I heard some of the guys talking about an explosion. It wasn't another bomb, was it?"

"I'll tell you this—Dotty was lucky she went looking for the cat as soon as she smelled smoke." Ava leaned over the table and lowered her voice. "And no, it wasn't a bomb. The fire started in the restroom just past Dotty's room. If she'd still been at that end of the building…"

Dotty was the last resident on that hall. A chill raced down Marie's arms, leaving goose bumps in its wake.

"So what caused it? A visitor sneaking a cigarette in the restroom?" The few residents who refused to quit knew they had to go outside for a smoke.

Ava shook her head. "The fire chief brought in an arson investigator from Boise. The fire was started deliberately. From what I understand, the guy started it with a liquid accelerant in the restroom between Dotty's room and the oxygen room. Apparently, when Hemlock Hills was built, the workers left small gaps between the floors and the bottom of the drywall sheets. And as the house shifted with ground settlement, the baseboards loosened too.

"So when the arsonist poured the accelerant, it flowed under the walls into the rooms on either side, taking the flames with it. The oxygen tanks began to overheat. They're still piecing it together, but they think the guy didn't realize that and opened the oxygen room door searching for an unlocked exit. A lot of the doors in there aren't marked because the Hills' manager was repainting. Before the arsonist could turn around and get out, the tanks started to explode from the increased pressure due to the heat. And when all that escaping oxygen hit the flames, kaboom." Ava imitated something blowing up with her hands.

"They think the body they found was the arsonist?"

"No doubt about it." Ava, still leaning across the table, waved Marie to lean in, too. "The arson investigator took some of the remains back to Boise with him. The Boise PD has one of those Rapid DNA machines that can develop a profile in less than two hours."

"Refill, ladies?" Vera stood over them, a coffeepot in one hand, the other planted on her hip.

Marie and Ava sat back in the booth while their cups were topped off.

"You two talking about that fire at the old folks home?"

Ava crinkled her forehead as if confused. "Hemlock Hills? Oh, no, I was telling Marie a story about my days in Chicago when I worked narcotics."

"Looked like it was pretty top secret, you ask me." Vera smirked.

"I was trying to keep my voice low so I wouldn't gross out anyone else." Ava stage-whispered to Vera, "I mean, who wants to eat breakfast while hearing about some guy who crammed so many vials of heroin up his—"

"I know you haven't been in town long, Officer Callan. But we don't allow that type of talk in here. If you want to continue enjoying our world-famous coffee and home cooking, I expect you to curb your graphic crime details."

"Yes, ma'am." Ava looked appropriately contrite until Vera stalked off toward the counter. Then she screwed her mouth to the side. "Dang it, Marie. Now I'm probably going to get sent to detention."

"Not my fault. I didn't say a word." Marie held her hands up in surrender. "But seriously, Ava, don't tell me anything that you shouldn't. I don't want to get you in trouble with Chief Walters."

Ava waved her in again and they resumed their heads-together positions. "There's going to be a press conference later today. You're just finding out a little sooner than most. But everyone on the force has been talking about it, so it's hardly confidential."

Thanking her lucky stars that Ava wasn't about to stop talking, Marie prompted, "So they ran a DNA test?"

"Yes. And based on the test results, they think the arsonist was that fugitive who was on the news this week. The guy who broke out of prison and was spotted near Twin Falls."

Stunned, Marie just blinked while emotions fought within her. Elation that Abel was dead. Guilt that he'd tried to kill Dotty to hurt Marie. Relief that she's safe. Dread that there might be more of Abel's accomplices still out there. Still coming for her. But with Abel dead and unable to direct anyone's actions, would they even bother with her now? Especially after all the attention directed at Jasper after the fire.

Oblivious to the turmoil raging inside Marie, Ava continued talking. "The forensic lab in Boise is convinced it's him, and they're turning the remains and evidence over to the FBI. Technically, it's their case, anyway." She leaned back, her brows drawing together. "Don't you think that's bizarre? A felon breaks out of prison and travels halfway across the country to set a nursing home on fire?"

Marie dropped her gaze to the tabletop. "Yeah, that's

weird all right." And why hadn't George or someone else from the Boise US Marshals' office been alerted to what was going on in Jasper? George's absence was becoming more and more puzzling. Marie had lost her faith in the WITSEC program. She was on her own.

Ava checked her watch. "I've gotta go. Catch the news tonight if you can. They'll probably have more details than I do."

"I will. And in the meantime, I promise not to repeat what you told me to anyone." Marie had been intent on finding out what she could, but not at the expense of Ava's career. That would have meant more guilt to pile on and carry around with all the rest.

"Don't worry. Like I said, it's unofficial, but not confidential." Ava slid to the edge of the booth and stood. "We should meet for lunch one of these days. I don't want Lacey's vet visits to be the only time we catch up."

"I'd love to. Give me a call when you know your schedule." Marie smiled to herself. Maybe now she could actually have friends to meet for lunch.

She paid her bill and left the diner. Instead of heading straight back to her office, Marie strolled to the town square and sat on a park bench. People rushed past on their way to work in downtown businesses. Shop owners unlocked their doors and flipped window signs from closed to open. Flowers planted throughout the park bloomed in a riot of colors.

With Abel gone, perhaps she could leave witness protection. She could continue on as Marie Beaumont since that's how everyone here already knew her. Or maybe she would reclaim her real identity, Megan Burnett. She'd have to make a pros-and-cons list to decide, but at least she had options now.

Well, not *right* now, but soon. She still needed to contact her case deputy. If not George, anyone would do. She wanted the go-ahead that she could leave the program. If she didn't hear from him soon, she'd drive down to Boise herself and take matters into her own hands.

How great would it be, not to have to lie anymore? To anyone. Without the lies, and now that she finally trusted Jack, maybe they could see where things went between them. After five lonely years, she was ready.

Marie's lips curved into a satisfied smile. Last night had been full of revelations, and aftershocks still swept through her, muscles tightening, other parts tingling. Like someone freed from prison, she'd luxuriated in the attention she'd received from Jack. A considerate lover, he'd taken things slow until she made it clear she'd already waited way too long.

His kindness to Dotty, his compassion for animals, his tenderness toward Marie, all sealed the deal. Despite her original apprehension about Jack, she felt at ease with him now. She wasn't at all ready for him to leave Jasper.

Leaning back against the bench, Marie inhaled a deep breath of fresh mountain air. Shifting her perception, she surveyed the town as if it were her home. A place where she belonged, with friends she could talk to. Not a place of exile, for a lifetime of loneliness and fear. On this glorious, sunny morning, anything seemed possible.

THE PRESS CONFERENCE Ava predicted had aired Thursday evening. The Boise stations all sent reporters and featured the story on their local five o'clock newscasts. The three main networks also mentioned it on their evening national news shows.

According to Liz, it had been the main topic of conversation everywhere in town on Friday. Marie took her word for it. Other than visiting Dotty at her temporary lodgings and delivering a wedding gift to Tashya, Marie had spent the day in the clinic. She'd avoided talking to people because her emotions were too extreme, too involved, too personal.

But now it was Saturday morning, and she was ready to let go of her tension and try for a little fun. If anyone could help her relax, it would be Jack. It was almost like they were the perfect couple, Marie trying to forget her past, Jack unable to remember his.

After parking in front of Emma's house, Marie released Astrid and hauled her duffel bag out of the SUV. Astrid started for the kennel and Marie called her back. "We're going in the house first, girl." Setting down her duffel, she crouched by Astrid and ran her hands through the dog's short hair. "While everyone is away this weekend for Jason and Tashya's wedding, we get to stay here and play with the animals."

"Can I be one of the animals you play with?" Jack stood in the open doorway, a huge grin splitting his face.

Marie's cheeks warmed as she straightened. Astrid whined, her big brown eyes bouncing between Marie and Jack as if watching a tennis match. Jack joined in. "Please can she come to me?"

"Honestly, between the two of you." Marie laughed. "Astrid, free."

Jack knelt and patted his chest. Astrid ran to him and soon they both went down in a pile of legs, arms and floppy ears.

Smiling, Marie sidled past them and took her bag to Emma's guest room. By the time she returned to the front door, Jack had disengaged himself from Astrid. He slid his arms around Marie and for a long moment they stared into each other's eyes. Leaning into him, she lowered her gaze to Jack's mouth. Traced his lips with her finger. Remembered the things his lips, his tongue, had done to her just a few nights ago.

Holding her against him with one arm, he cradled her cheek and tipped her face up toward his. As his lips touched hers, barely a whisper of contact, every nerve ending in her body sizzled. Marie rose on her tiptoes, intent on capturing his mouth. But Jack pulled back, making her wait. Driving her crazy. By the time his gentle kisses turned demanding, Marie met them with equal force. When they finally separated, Marie gasped for breath as her legs trembled.

"Are we sure we want to go rafting today?" Jack's wicked grin made her laugh.

"Yes, we're definitely going rafting." Marie looked down at Astrid, who'd been watching them kiss. "But not you, girl. You're staying home today."

"I've rarely seen you without her."

Marie walked out to the porch with Astrid. "I don't want to worry about her falling in the river."

As they all headed to the kennel, Astrid's head and tail hung down.

"I don't think she's happy about it." Jack pointed out the obvious.

Marie put Astrid in the same stall as Amaya and the puppies. "You two behave." Marie squatted and loved up Astrid.

As they closed the kennel door, a forlorn howl started up and Jack's eyes widened in mock horror.

Marie laughed. "That's the beagle part of her."

Jack wrinkled his nose and chuckled. "Now I see why you don't leave her behind much. What a racket."

"I know, right?" Marie laughed along with him, even though howling wasn't why she usually never left Astrid behind. But for the first time in a long while, Marie felt safe not taking Astrid with her. Especially with Jack at her side. "Just don't tell *her*. I think it might hurt her feelings."

"If hurt feelings sound like that, not a problem."

Marie drove them through town toward Blaze's River Tours and Rafting. The morning was fair, a warm sun and a blue sky dotted with hundreds of fluffy white clouds. As they drew near the popular rafting spot, the crowds increased. Marie peered in the rearview mirror at the empty backseat. No Astrid. She suddenly felt exposed and agitated, scanning the crowd for someone who didn't belong, someone paying too much attention to her.

"Have you done much rafting?" Jack asked.

She exhaled. Slowly, so Jack wouldn't notice. Abel was dead. Her life had become her own again. She made a concerted effort to smile and relax her grip on the steering wheel. "I'm not much of a swimmer, but I've gone a few times, though only on Class II and III runs, and only with a guide. Class IV, or heaven forbid a Class V, no way, not ever. Every year it seems at least one or two people die on one of those excursions, and I have no intention of that being me." *Not with the kind of luck I have.*

"Then thanks for trusting me."

Marie drove around until she found a parking spot. "Come to think about it, why is that? Why am I trusting you, that is?" She turned off the engine and climbed out.

Jack unbuckled, got out and stared at her across the top of the RAV4. "I'm going to tell you why."

"First," Marie countered, jabbing her index finger in the air, "you're going to stop staring at me like that." Those eyes. Worse than any Siren's song. If she was going to get on the water, she needed her wits.

Jack shrugged, tipping his head and grinning in a way that could only be described as charmingly arrogant. "Like what?" he asked, all innocent-like.

"As if you didn't know, Mr. Hypnotic Staring Man."

Jack burst out laughing. "Seriously?"

"I'm not kidding. Cut it out or I'm not going."

"Okay, okay. How's this?" He crossed his eyes.

"Ha-ha, funny man."

"Well, if I'm Mr. Hypnotic Staring Man, you must

be Miss Chicken to Get on the Water and Using Any Excuse Possible Not To. Nice to meet you."

Marie rolled her eyes, slammed the front car door closed and got her bag from the backseat. "Remind me again why I'm trusting you?"

"The more I flipped through my rafting magazines, the more sure I became that I've done it before." Jack followed suit and retrieved his bag. "So yesterday, I rode Ol' Blue down to the river and watched for a while. And guess what?"

"Ol' Blue?"

"My bike."

"You named your bike Ol' Blue?"

"He's blue. I wasn't going to name him Ol' Red." Jack drummed his fingers on the car roof. "Stop changing the subject. Are you gonna guess or what?"

"No. Just tell me."

"Spoilsport. I had some memory flashes. And they didn't bring on a headache. It seems like happy memories and things I remember that didn't actually happen to *me*, don't hurt me at all. Anyway, I've done this before. Rafting, I mean. Kayaking, too. Lots of times. But I wanted to be sure. So Blaze and I had a long talk. Great guy, by the way. Heard all about his problem with that bomber. Told me you saved the life of one of the heroes who helped catch the guy."

Marie frowned. "Ava's dog, Lacey. Yeah. Terrible what happened to her, but she pulled through."

"Thanks to you."

"I had something to do with it, sure." She shook her head as she remembered. "But that dog. She had one strong will to live. Amaya reminds me of her. But what did you learn from Mr. Blaze?"

As he spoke, Marie couldn't help but be infected by Jack's enthusiasm. That stare of his changed. His eyes became animated, sparkling with pleasure and his grin was warm and genuine. "That's the thing. When he started talking, I knew what he was talking about. You know, things like eddy fence, throw bags, dry bags, swimmers."

"What're all those things? I don't know what *you're* talking about."

Jack chuckled. "An eddy fence is the swirly water line between an eddy and the current. A throw bag is a piece of rescue equipment, and a dry bag is just what it sounds like. It keeps water out and hopefully keeps the stuff you put in it dry."

"And swimmers? People swim down these rapids?"

Jack hoisted his bag over one shoulder. "No. Well, not that I know about. A swimmer means someone who has fallen out of the raft."

"That's not going to happen to me, right?" Marie held her bag by the straps and met him around the back of the vehicle. Together they headed for Blaze's.

"No, and that's why Blaze and I decided that a tandem kayak would suit us better than a raft. Easier for us to control by ourselves."

"Why don't we go with a guide?"

They edged their way inside the newly opened Blaze's River Tours and Rafting, crowded with people checking in, gearing up, slathering on sunblock.

"A kayak can be more fun. And we don't need a

guide. I'll be your guide." He puffed out his chest in a comical pose.

"Jack!" Blaze hollered from across the room and barreled his way through the throng. "You made it, and with the vet in tow. Good, good. Got your gear all set." He turned to Marie and grabbed both her hands in his. "So glad to see you." He squeezed her hands and then let her go. "It's a great morning to be on the river. You're going to love the pools between the rapids, with waters deep enough to soothe the soul. And then the drops, where the rapids pick up again and are the real reason you're here. Water temps are warm, so you won't need to rent wet suits."

"Just as you predicted," Jack said.

Blaze placed his finger on his nose. "I've got a nose for it. And you're in luck with Jack, here. Knows his stuff," Blaze said to Marie with a firm nod of his head. "He'll be a fine guide."

"Glad to hear it." *Because her life would be in his hands.*

Blaze turned to Jack. "Stow your gear in the lockers over there. I've got you a dry bag already packed, and the shuttle bus is arranged for your return trip. When you reach the bottom, look for the bus named Greenleaf. They'll be expecting you. Your kayak is already in the water out back. Head that way," he said, pointing. "You can pick up your PFD and other gear, then you're off. Now, go! Enjoy your day."

Marie gave Jack a quizzical look. "PFD?"

He grinned. "It's the term we professionals use for a personal flotation device."

"Professional, huh? Well, thanks for the education. And Jack?" She waited until he met her eyes.

"Yeah?"

"Thanks for this day," she said, and she meant it. She couldn't remember the last time she felt this relaxed and excited at the same time, the last time she allowed herself a whole day for nothing but fun.

"You're welcome." There was a weight of meaning behind the soft reply.

"Oh, Jack. I forgot to mention," Blaze said, stopping them. "Make sure you're off the river by midafternoon. Weather report says those fluffy little darlings outside are going to form up. Predicting severe thunderstorms this evening."

"Good to know," Jack said, seemingly unconcerned.

"Got to run." And like his name, the owner was gone in a blaze.

Marie stopped in her tracks. "Thunderstorms. Um, maybe—"

"Don't even think about backing out. Come on. Everything's going to be fine."

Jack took charge. He saw to it that they were outfitted with life jackets, full-cut helmets and neoprene booties for their feet.

"The water is nice when you're out in the sun," he explained. "But your feet will probably be wet the whole time. I think paying a little extra for these makes for a more enjoyable ride."

"You *think*, do you? I'm not going to ask you about all these memories just now, but I reserve the right to question you about them later."

"And I promise to tell you everything, even though I have no clue how I'm remembering some of these things." He shrugged.

He helped Marie get into the front seat and showed her the handles along the edges of the kayak. "If you fall out, just grab on to one of these or the side of the kayak, and I'll pull you back in."

"That in no way reassures me."

He laughed, and it was rich and full-bodied. "Stop worrying." He handed her a paddle, grabbed the dry bag and got situated in the back.

"That's not in my nature."

"How about you try it for just one day? Heck, how about for just a few hours?"

She twisted around and gave him a fake, cheesy smile. "Here you go. This is me, totally not worried."

"Whoa. Now, I'm the one who's not reassured."

"Not so easy, eh? Hey, listen, I've only kayaked once in my whole life, and it was by myself on a very small lake. I'm not sure how two-person rowing works."

"Tandem works the same way. We paddle together, same side at the same time. If we need to maneuver around anything, I'll make the calls."

"Aye aye, Captain." Marie gave him a sharp salute.

They practiced in the calm water at the launch point until Marie felt comfortable with the motion and paddling. Then they traveled across the river and entered the downstream current, the rapids easy, with still pools between.

Marie tipped her face toward the sky, smiling at the sun. She was happy. Safe. And her feelings for Jack?

They went way beyond like, and unless she was off the mark, he seemed to feel the same way.

Drifting farther downstream, they hit a few spots that made Marie's heart skip a beat, but Jack kept control of the kayak, and except for his occasional shouted directions, the hustle and splash of the river made conversation difficult. They were getting tossed around a little, but Jack worked to keep them away from large rocks.

Farther down the river there would be a fork on their left that led to a Class V run. Just the idea of the chaotic water, crashing as waves against rocks and forming whirlpools with deadly undercurrents, made her queasy.

But Marie relaxed in the knowledge that Jack knew what he was doing. He'd promised to take care of her, and she trusted him. She looked back at him and smiled. He raised his oar and grinned back.

Today was going to be a fantastic day.

Chapter Fourteen

As soon as Jack was in the water with the paddle in his hands, muscle memory kicked in. If he felt comfortable on the river, sitting in the kayak was like coming home. His lost memories weren't coming to him in a rush; they were creeping in. At least the pleasant ones were, and the joy he derived from challenging the river filled him.

As for the rest? Jack pushed aside thoughts of the nightmares that still came every night. The flashes of that one, horrific scene in the West Virginia woods where Abel Gaines had his shootout with law enforcement. Jack even pushed aside the possibility that he'd been on Abel's payroll. According to the news, Abel Gaines was dead, and as far as Jack was concerned, whatever his connection to the terrorist might have been, it was just as dead.

Instead, he cast his eyes on Marie sitting in front of him. A rope of braided hair came out of the bottom of her helmet, its tip resting at the edge of her pink tank top. Well-toned shoulder blades moved easily as she paddled. She seemed happier than he'd seen her, and

he was willing to take at least partial credit for her relaxed mood. Making love to her had rocked his world,
and he was pretty confident it had rocked hers, too.

So today would be about her, about teaching her
to relax and just have a little fun. Then maybe, just
maybe, she would relent and open up to him. To that
aim, yesterday he and Blaze had mapped out the route
he would take. About an hour from now, he would take
the right fork at Push-off Rock to avoid the Class V.

In the meantime, this day would also be about him.
He needed to relax as much as Marie did, and he con-
centrated on the muscle burn from paddling. He enjoyed
the clear water, wide pools and drops that nature pro-
vided. He laughed out loud when they roller-coastered
through the splashy waves.

As he navigated the river, taking in the wilderness
of steep hillsides, deep gorges and dense forests, the
peace and quiet of the atmosphere brought forth another memory. In his mind, a man was speaking. At
first, he couldn't quite remember who, but then the
story formed clearly in his head.

One evening during World War II, Winston
Churchill was dining at 10 Downing Street when the
air raid sirens went off. Allegedly, his gut warned him
of impending danger, and he told his staff to leave the
kitchen immediately. A short time later, a bomb landed
exactly where his staff had been.

Like Churchill, Jack's gut began to churn. His grip
on the paddle tightened as he scanned the river. No
seams, where two currents flowing in opposite directions meet and form an unstable line in the current.

No keeper holes, thank God. The powerful backwash of one of those could suck a kayak in and keep recirculating it until long after the rider drowned. Nothing at all to give him pause. He looked to his right, then left, checking each riverbank. Nothing there, either. Glancing up, he checked out the heights on either side of the river. Nothing.

What could have possibly set his senses on high alert?

The oar suddenly jerked in his hand, so hard that he nearly lost his grip. At the same time, a piece of plastic from the paddle splintered off and hit him in the face. He felt the sting on his cheek. "What the...?"

In the hills to his right, he saw a glint of sun reflecting off something. But no noise followed the hit of his paddle, like he'd expect if it had been a gunshot. Had he somehow snagged his oar under a rock without realizing it? He didn't think so, but that made more sense than someone shooting at them.

The current took them near a rock jutting up to the left. Push-off Rock, Blaze had informed Jack. The marker just before the fork. If he pushed off the rock to its right, they would continue down the easy Class II, which was exactly where they wanted to go.

Go around the rock on its left, and they'd enter the foaming rush of the Class V. In an inflatable kayak. With an inexperienced rider. And Jack with a damaged paddle. That was where they definitely *didn't* want to go.

As they approached the rock, Jack held his paddle in both hands and leaned toward it. Just then, a bullet sheared off a slice of stone right in front of his face. It sailed across the kayak and into the river. Once again, he couldn't hear anything. The shooter was using a suppressor.

Jack dug his oar into the water, twisting his torso to add more torque. The bow of the kayak edged to the left, and he didn't have time to explain to Marie why their course was changing.

"Jack!" Marie screamed.

They weren't on a Class II anymore.

THE INSTANT THE kayak committed to the Class V fork of the Salmon, Marie knew she was going to die. Her mind swirled with possibilities. Abel might be dead, but apparently not all his followers were. Abel had escaped with the help of others. He had been seen at the Idaho-Utah border in the company of another man. Jack had an airtight alibi for both; he'd already been in town then. But someone had to locate her for Abel, and Jack *could* be that someone.

Jack was going to kill her. What other explanation could there be? He'd lulled her with honeyed words and sweet lovemaking so she'd lower her guard. Then, when Abel had died, Jack must have decided to finish the job for him. He took her to the one place where he could be guaranteed to get away with killing her.

She had to be some kind of deeply flawed individual to yet again miss seeing a man for who he really was. Didn't matter that Emma had missed seeing it. Dotty, too. Even Astrid had missed it.

Already, the kayak was being tossed around in ways that frightened the hell out of her. She chanced a quick look behind her. Jack's biceps bulged as he paddled like a mad man, fighting to keep them upright. She turned forward again. When the kayak lurched to the left, Marie shrieked, slid her paddle under her feet and grabbed hold of the edge of the kayak. They spun in a circle, a vortex grabbing hold and threatening to pull them under. They finally broke free and shot forward. Straight into the middle of the Class V.

"No!" she screamed. They spun between rocks the size of cars. They bounced over waves and dropped down, getting swamped. Then they were caught up in a spot where two different currents battled for control. It pulled them to the aerated backwash of what looked like a recirculating geyser that exploded upward, then sucked back into itself.

Jack yelled something at her, but she couldn't make it out. She looked over her shoulder.

He yelled again, and again his words drifted away. He held up his paddle, and for the first time she saw that it was broken. He pointed at his, then hers, then himself.

Marie could handle a lot without losing it. But apparently, Class V rapids, the betrayal by Jack and a fear of dying pushed her past reason.

I'll give you my paddle, all right. She picked it up and swung it at him. Only a quick last-minute duck saved him from a blow to the head and perhaps losing his memories for good this time. Jack managed to grab hold of the handle and yanked it out of her hand.

Almost losing her balance, Marie faced forward, grabbing the sides of the kayak again. They hit the hole she'd seen, where the water flowed over rocks and toward the bottom of the river, then reversed onto itself in an eruption of whitewater.

The kayak went airborne. Her grip on the sides slipped and when the kayak dropped, Marie sailed forward over the bow and into the river.

And like a dog with a new toy, the river played with her. It sucked her beneath its surface and trapped her there until her lungs threatened to explode. She broke free and came up sputtering and coughing out water.

She managed to get her legs out straight in front of her, the safest way to go downstream. But the river tugged her sideways, then spun her, slamming her head into a rock. Her full-cut helmet protected her brain as her head bounced against the foam padding.

Straightening her legs on top of the water again, arms crossed over her chest like a corpse, Marie shot down the rapids, cursing every smack into a rock, every plunge beneath the surface. Where the loop reconnected to the main branch, churning waters shot her into a still pool halfway across the river.

Marie swam to the far bank and dragged herself out of the water, gasping for air. Although her arms hung like broken rubber bands at her sides, she worked her helmet off and unbuckled her life jacket. After resting a minute on her back, she stood. Shaky, but her legs would hold her.

It was happening to her again. The man she cared about was trying to kill her.

JACK'S FEAR AS he fought the rapids was nothing compared to seeing the bow seat empty. "Marie!" His gaze swept over the churning water; he was hoping for a glimpse of her head or her arms flailing in the spray. Not even a spot of neon yellow from her vest was in sight.

Was she held captive beneath the power of the swirling water, subjected to a slow death by drowning?

"Maa-riee!" Her name hung in the air for a moment before the furious rapids swallowed it, just as they'd swallowed her. Jack bent to the paddle and maneuvered out of the hole that had trapped them. The kayak lurched forward. He tried in vain to stop his downstream momentum so he could find her.

You idiot.

With her body weighing less than the kayak, Marie had likely cascaded down the river and could be as much as a half mile ahead of him already. He paddled for all he was worth, constantly scouting for signs of her.

Why had she tried to hit him with her paddle? True, she most likely didn't know they were being fired upon or that he was trying to save their lives. Even he couldn't hear the shots, and by the time he was sure, they were on the part of the river where you couldn't hear yourself think, let alone talk. He'd sworn there'd be no rough rapids, yet they wound up on a Class V. When she'd turned around and looked at him, the naked hatred on her face had stunned him.

He battled to stay upright as the tumultuous water swept him around a bend. The main river banked left, and Jack shot through the last dangerous whirlpool and into still water. Pushing past his exhaustion, he paddled to the thin crescent of sandy beach closest to him. He stumbled out of the craft, his overworked muscles cramping until he fell forward on his hands and knees. Scrambling up, he grabbed the kayak and pulled it out of the water. A few yards up the beach sat a large boulder formation. He ran for it, climbed and scoured the river. No neon yellow life jacket or helmet.

A cauldron of fear and anger, like the river itself, bubbled through his veins. She blamed him. Of course, she did. He'd promised to keep her safe, and he'd failed. Completely. He'd made the wrong call, steering them away from the shooter. By trying to save her life, had he sentenced her to death?

Cursing his lack of a cell phone, he slid down the rocks and ran back to the kayak. Where was the dry bag? There was a flare inside.

"No!" Just like Marie, the bag was gone. Miles from here by now, or buried in the underwater silt.

He pushed the kayak back into the water and leaped in. The landing area couldn't be much farther. The faster he got there, the faster he could report her missing, and the faster the police could start hunting for whoever had targeted him from the hills.

Abel Gaines was dead, but clearly someone connected to him nursed a grudge against Jack. He paddled hard, ignoring the pain of his overexertion. All this time, he'd worried about the wrong thing, so sure he was a man with a violent past. Not once did it occur to him that he might not be the perpetrator of violence, but the target. Possibly both. Anyone foolish enough

Chapter Fifteen

Concealed in the shade of a pine tree, Marie peeked between its branches, searching for Jack. A bright flash of orange caught her eye, their kayak coming out of the same loop where she had. But instead of paddling toward her, Jack swung around to beach on the far side of the river.

Marie turned around and leaned her back against the tree. Curling her fingers into fists, she pounded them against her thighs.

Stupid, stupid, stupid.

Even the extra rules she lived by now hadn't prevented a repeat of her worst mistake. She'd been attracted to Abel's charm and intelligence. He'd treated her with respect. Until she'd walked into his war room, its walls covered with maps, pictures of government buildings and whiteboards detailing bomb attacks, she'd even thought he might be the one.

And here she was again. Charmed by Jack, already falling for him. The first man in years she'd kissed, let alone made love with. Inhaling a cleansing breath,

Marie stopped chastising herself. She shifted her focus back to surviving.

Another glimpse through the branches revealed Jack digging through the kayak. Marie seized the opportunity to skedaddle.

The beach area on her side of the river ended at a gentle slope of trees and plants. Working her way upriver and upslope at the same time, Marie used trees for cover as she climbed toward safety.

Sorry, not sorry, Jack. Today's not my day to die.

MARIE PULLED HERSELF up over the edge of the slope. The road lay just beyond the trees, and she trudged toward the landing spot downriver, hoping someone there could give her a lift back to her SUV at Blaze's. A glance at the sky, filling with dark storm clouds, made her hustle.

More people than she'd expected milled around at the landing. Two police cars were parked just off the road, and she made her way down to where the cops were talking to some men.

"What's happened?" she asked. As all eyes turned toward her, Marie looked down at her bedraggled appearance.

A river guide came over to her. "What happened to *you*?"

Unwilling to involve anyone else in this mess, and having no proof that Jack tried to kill her, Marie shrugged. "I fell out. Lost my grip and over I went."

"Were you on a raft?" The guide seemed upset that she might have been left behind by a Blaze employee.

"No, a kayak. The friend I went with is still on the river with it. I'm sure he'll be here any minute." She needed to get out of here before Jack showed up. Figure out how to protect herself. "I'm sorry to put you to any trouble, but could one of you give me a ride back to Blaze's, where I'm parked?"

One of the police officers stepped closer. "I'm Officer Hampton, ma'am. I'd be happy to give you a lift."

Thanking him, Marie climbed into the squad car with Hampton. As he reached the road and turned north, Marie looked through her window at the river. An orange kayak approached the landing area.

As soon as Jack learned she was alive, he'd be coming after her again.

But this time she'd be ready.

And this time *he* wouldn't see it coming.

As Jack beached the kayak, he noticed a police officer talking to one of the Blaze guides. Jack rushed over and interrupted them.

"My friend fell out of our kayak and I couldn't find her. We need to start a search right away. Someone was shoo—"

"Whoa, slow down, buddy," the cop said. "Take it from the top, but calmly."

Jack gave the guide a pleading look. "Please, if we don't find her soon, I'm afraid it'll be too late."

"What's her name?" the guide asked.

"Marie Beaumont. She flipped out as we were—"

"I know Marie. You can calm down. She was just here, and she's fine."

Jack didn't know whether to laugh, cry or kiss the guide. "You're sure? She's all right?"

"A little waterlogged, but she seemed fine otherwise."

The officer stepped away and keyed his shoulder mic. Static crackled over an unintelligible reply. "Hey, Jenny, what's the name of the guy you wanted me to bring in?"

"Jack." This time the dispatcher's voice came through loud and clear.

"Hang on a second," the cop said to his shoulder. Then to Jack, "Hey, buddy, what's your name?"

"Who wants to know?" Jack's relief that Marie was alive deflated with the police wanting to know who he was.

The mic squawked again.

"What, Jenny?"

Jenny's voice crackled to life again. "If it's Jack, you need to bring him in to the station, Nugent."

"Why?" Jack asked.

Officer Nugent let go of his mic. "You heard the lady. Let's go."

"You don't even know if I'm the person she wants."

"You're the guy with amnesia, aren't you?" This from the river guide.

The cop was paying attention. "Unless you show me some ID that proves you're not Jack, I'm taking you in."

"You can't just—"

"I *can* just." Nugent unhooked his cuffs from his belt. "Come on, buddy. Don't make me use these." He waggled the handcuffs in his hand.

Jack backed away from the cop, who grabbed Jack's arms, pulled them behind his back and cuffed him. Jack found himself being put in the backseat of the squad car.

The day Jack awoke with amnesia had been the most frustrating day of his life, until now. Today, Marie disappeared but was apparently safe. The police wanted him at the station but wouldn't tell him why.

He pushed the pieces around like a giant jigsaw puzzle. His nightmares and jagged memories. Recognizing Abel Gaines's picture. The certainty of a connection between himself and Marie. Jack's worst guesses as to his identity seemed to be coming true.

He'd been one of Abel's lackeys, here to do the fugitive's dirty work for him.

And he was about to wind up behind bars.

Chapter Sixteen

Officer Nugent marched Jack into the police station, arms still cuffed behind his back. Memories of other police stations, or similar places, poked at Jack's mind. Smells of paper, mold, gun oil and leather. And always the hint of either urine or vomit. Stabbing pain tore at the backs of his eyes.

Just when he thought the unpleasantness of his past was over with, something came along and triggered the damn headaches. Was he doomed to suffer these for the rest of his life?

He was escorted across the lobby floor just as a uniformed Asian woman stormed out from behind the front desk.

"Why is this man cuffed?"

"Jenny, you told me to bring him in, so I brought him in."

"Bring him in, sure, but I never said anything about cuffs. Get those off of him this minute." Then to Jack, "So sorry about this. I guess you know almost everyone in the department is in McCall for Jason's wedding. Some of the McCall cops were kind enough to volunteer to cover the weekend shifts. But what can I say?" She shrugged apologetically.

Nugent stepped behind Jack to remove his cuffs.

"It happens," Jack said, but he wasn't sure it did. "You must be Jenny Dix." At her raised brows, he added, "Jason mentioned you."

"Ah. Yes, Officer Dix, at your service. Call me Jenny."

With the cuffs removed, Jack rotated his shoulders and rubbed his wrists. "Well, Jenny, at the moment, you're my new favorite person. You want to tell me why I was brought in?"

"Not here. Follow me. Nugent, watch the desk for me. I'll be right back." She led Jack through a bullpen to a small interview room. "Have a seat. I have something for you."

Jack dropped into a chair. Resting his arms on the table, he folded his hands and closed his eyes. Taking deep breaths, he readied himself for whatever came next.

Less than a minute later, Jenny returned, carrying a box, which she carefully set on the table. It was a used supply box, brown with old shipping labels on the outside. The top flaps were bent, some frayed at the edges. Not a box he would associate with the care Jenny was taking in handling it.

She took the chair opposite Jack, placing one hand on the top of the box. Employing the compassionate tone used to convey horrible news to crime victims, she asked, "Does the name Finnegan mean anything to you?"

Jack clenched his jaw. "Should it?"

"Maybe not yet, but it will." Jenny smiled. "It's your last name."

They'd found out who he was. Jack Finnegan. The two names together nudged a corner of his brain.

And Jenny had ordered cuffs removed. He wasn't wanted, then. Not a known associate of Abel Gaines. Jack felt the tension in his shoulders give.

"It almost sounds familiar. But I…how do you know it's my name?"

"This morning a hiker came in. He'd been hiking the gully below where you were found, and he came across a black pickup truck. It was pancaked, apparently from falling off the cliff above it." Jenny stood and opened the box flaps. "Inside the truck, he found your duffel bag. When I looked through it, I realized it belonged to you and sent Nugent to find you at the river."

A pickup truck. Duffel bag. Finnegan.

"How did you know I'd be at the river?"

Jenny shrugged. "Small town. I'm going to give you privacy to go through this. I'm not sure if it will help you remember, or what'll happen if you do, but if you need anything, I'll be right outside."

"Thanks." *I think.*

I hope.

"Listen, maybe it's none of my business, but I think you'll be happy with what you find." She closed the door behind her when she left.

Jack stood and looked down in the box. Inside was a duffel, coated with dried mud. He opened it. Lying on top of soggy, mildewed clothes was a wallet. He removed it and sat back down to go through its contents. Everything was damp, so he worked with care to not rip anything.

A Washington driver's license with Jack's picture. Address in Seattle. "Jack Finnegan." It rolled off his tongue in a familiar way. Credit cards in his name. A couple pictures stuck together. The top one was of a woman, two young girls and a young boy. Pain, like a sword through his chest, gripped him. He recognized his mom and sisters, all murdered by Jack's father.

Also in the duffel, a leather case, which Jack pulled out. He flipped it open. And almost dropped it. A deputy US marshal badge. The ID proved it belonged to him.

He cradled his forehead in his hands as an onslaught of memories came from all directions. He was a freaking deputy US marshal. Not part of Abel Gaines's crew. What he knew of the shootout in West Virginia was from the law enforcement side.

Marie! He no longer had to hold back his feelings for her, thinking he had a criminal past. Jack opened the door and Jenny appeared.

"Everything all right?" she asked, her brows drawn together in concern.

"Better than all right. Thank you for finding me as soon as you could. But before I leave, I'd like to file a report. I don't have much information, so I'm not sure if it'll even do any good, but I'd rather have a record of it."

"Sure. What type of report?"

"While Marie and I were kayaking today, someone shot at us from the top of a cliff. Hit the end of my paddle, and then just missed us again when he hit the rock we were next to." Jack touched his cheek where the piece of his oar had hit him.

"That's awful. Is Marie okay?" Jenny waved at him to follow her to her desk.

"He didn't hit us." Not exactly answering the question, since he doubted Marie was what he'd call okay.

Jenny took down what little information Jack could give her. "Well, it's not much to go on, but I'll get someone out there as soon as I can to check for shell casings, any other possible evidence. Might have been stray bullets from a hunter, but he shouldn't have been aiming at the river. I'll let Fish and Game know too so they can keep an eye out for hunters on those cliffs, just in case."

"Thanks." Jack hoped Jenny was right and the shooter hadn't been targeting him. But the idea that he'd almost caused Marie to drown for no reason made him sick to his stomach. "Is there a chance someone can give me a ride to the DCA?"

"Officer Nugent's about to go off the clock. He can take you on his way home." She followed Jack into the room while he picked up the box. "Your gun was in the truck, too. The hiker found it on the floor of the cab, packed with mud. We're hanging on to it for now. The chief needs to release firearms himself."

"No problem. The last thing I need right now is a gun."

Chapter Seventeen

As predicted, the early evening Idaho sky turned gun-metal gray from the buildup of massive thunderclouds. In the distance, Marie saw the flicker of fork lightning, and the wind, which had been quiet all day, kicked up a notch. The day's warmth fell away, and the heavy scent of rain permeated the air. Like a soldier on the eve of battle, Marie was beset both internally and externally by forbidding expectations, adrenaline shakes and a roiling stomach.

A plume of dust alerted her that someone headed her way. Her pulse ramped up and she rubbed her sweat-damp palms on her jeans. She didn't want to shoot Jack. She just wanted him to go away, get arrested, whatever it took to get him out of her life.

She'd been sitting cross-legged on top of the RV, waiting. Now she swung her legs behind her and lay on her stomach near the front edge of the vehicle, positioning Emma's loaded Winchester so she could look through the scope.

She may have been fooled by Jack's good guy routine, but she had no intention of playing the meek victim. Emma kept the rifle to scare off coyotes and the occasional mountain lion. Marie was using it to scare off a snake. A yellow-bellied, two-legged snake.

Whose kisses were sweet as cotton candy.

"Bring it, Jack," she muttered, her anger stoked when remembering how the day had begun. What a fool she'd been.

Pressing the stock snug against her shoulder, Marie squinted, sighting the red compact car as it came through the DCA's front gate and up the long dirt drive.

Her two-legged snake sat in the passenger seat, leaning forward to peer out the windshield. "You can't see me, but I can see you," she murmured. She placed him in the crosshairs. "If you think you're going to catch me unaware a second time, you've got another think coming."

She didn't recognize the driver. Maybe one of Abel's men, maybe some unwitting person who'd picked up a hitchhiker. She'd worry about him later. As the car stopped in the circular drive, facing the RV and barn, Marie turned her head and shouted down to her backup. "Astrid, stay." She'd positioned the dog at the rear of the RV where the ladder was located so no one could climb up without her knowledge.

The passenger door swung open.

Her pulse ramped up.

Jack stepped out of the vehicle.

After leaning back in to speak to the driver, he closed the door and walked to the trunk, which popped open. Jack carried a large brown box around to the driver's window and spoke to the other man again, then headed toward the RV.

Marie aimed the rifle. Wrapped her finger around the trigger. Inhaled. Blew out half her breath and pulled the trigger.

The kick was painful, hard and sharp. Her ears rang. The bullet hit the dirt in front of Jack, spraying him with dust, the report echoing like thunder.

He dropped the box and slithered like the snake he was to the passenger-side door, pulled it open and crouched behind it. At the same time, the driver tumbled out of his side and followed suit, but unlike Jack, he aimed a gun at her.

She hadn't counted on that.

"Marie!" Jack shouted, looking around as if he didn't know exactly where she was.

"I've got you in my crosshairs, Jack, and my first shot was just a warning. If I'd wanted to hit you, you better believe I would have. Now, get back in that car and leave." Her voice carried in the quiet evening air.

Jack's face contorted in feigned confusion. "Crosshairs? Marie, are you the one shooting at me?"

What an actor.

She fired again. "How's that for an answer? I want you and your minion out of here. I mean it!"

"Marie, for God's sake, tell me what's going on!"

That was rich. "You tried to kill me today."

"You mean the river? That's not what happened."

"You're a liar. I'm only going to tell you one more time. Leave."

"Give me one minute and I can clear all of this up."

"I'm not—"

The driver held up his hand. "Marie, I'm Officer Nugent of the McCall Police Department. I need you to put down the gun and come down from up there with your hands up." In a quieter voice, she heard him ask Jack, "Did you try to kill her on the river?"

"No! Someone was shooting at us. I filed a report with Jenny when I was at the station."

Marie turned the scope on the officer and saw the badge he held.

"I don't believe either one of you."

"Marie, he's a real cop." Cautiously, Jack straightened to a standing position. He spoke to her as if she were a skittish, cornered animal. "They found my personal effects from the night of the storm. Jenny, the dispatcher, gave them to me this afternoon. My name is Jack Finnegan and I'm a deputy US marshal." He moved out from behind the car door, hands up.

She couldn't believe she was waffling. "Prove it."

Jack walked to the box he'd dropped and pulled out a badge. He held it up, but she could make out little more than its shape. Could be from a box of Cracker Jack for all she knew.

"Don't move." Marie pulled her phone from her back pocket. She found the main number for the marshals' office in Boise. At the after-hours recording, she punched the option to speak to a live person. When the operator came on the line, Marie asked to speak to Jack Finnegan.

"Who's calling?"

"It doesn't matter who I am. I need to know if there's a Jack Finnegan there."

"Ma'am, I'm sorry, but I can't provide information on whether someone is or isn't an employee. If you'd like to leave a message—"

Dang it. Marie hung up. She'd gone through the same routine when she'd tried reaching George through the main number.

"Ma'am?" the "cop" called out from behind the safety of his car door. His gun was still trained on her. "Call the Jasper PD. Ask to speak with Jenny. She can confirm what we've been telling you."

Why not? Marie dialed the number.

"Jasper Police Department. Is this an emergency?"

"Is this Jenny? It's Dr. Beaumont."

"Marie? What can I do for you?"

"I have a question for you. What is Jack with-no-memory's last name?"

"Oh, you haven't heard." Excitement colored Jenny's voice. "We recovered his personal belongings. His name's Jack Finnegan. Turns out he's a deputy US marshal. Can you believe it?"

"Jenny, I can't explain right now, but my life depends on how sure you are that he's legit."

"Are you all right? Do you need—"

"I'm fine. I just need to confirm he's with the Marshals Service."

"Yes, he's legit. I went through his things before we brought him in, to make sure who they belonged to. I recognized his picture on his driver's license. I even ran a check on him to make sure, and his record is stellar."

"Thanks, Jenny. I appreciate it. I promise I'm okay, and I'll talk to you later."

Not sure if she should be embarrassed, still wary or just plain relieved, Marie climbed down the RV's ladder. But she kept hold of the Winchester and commanded Astrid to heel as she confronted the two men.

Officer Nugent already had his badge and ID out to show her. "You mind putting the rifle down?"

Marie thanked him and set the rifle on the ground. Nugent talked to each of them separately, finally satisfied that both were okay and neither intended to shoot the other.

"Well, it seems you two will resolve this with a conversation, so I'm going to take off. The weather looks like it's about to turn nasty."

"Sure," Jack said, looking to the sky. "Thanks for the lift."

Nugent shook his head, chuckling. "No, thank you. Most interesting day I've had in a while."

Marie shrugged. "I had to be sure. You understand."

"Not the details, but I'm sure you two will sort things out."

Marie nodded, and Nugent climbed in his car, waving as he drove off.

She remained standing where she'd been, staring at Jack. Apparently, there was a limit to how many emotions she could deal with at one time before being rendered speechless and brain dead. Astrid whined and looked up at her, but Marie wasn't quite ready to release her.

Jack's intense gaze looked haunted. "I'll explain

what happened on the river today, then you can tell me why on earth you thought I wanted to kill you. But first, can I show you my stuff?"

Blowing out a long breath, Marie picked up the rifle and put it in safe mode. "You use that line on all the ladies?"

Chuckling, he picked up the box. "Nope. You're the first one. And hopefully the last."

That brought a smile to her lips.

"Let's go in the RV. Nugent was right, looks like it's about to rain." There was a hesitancy to Jack's steps as he walked over to her. Astrid looked up at him, issuing a low growl and wagging her tail at the same time. "And maybe call off your enforcer? I'd like to keep all my appendages. Especially the ones at chomping height."

"Astrid, free." Marie waved her hand toward Jack. "Free."

Jack held his hand out for Astrid to sniff. "Just until she knows for sure I'm not the bad guy."

Twisting her mouth to the side, Marie snickered. "She knows. She knew before I did."

"Good girl, Astrid." Jack knelt on one knee, set the box back down and patted his chest. Astrid was on him in a flash, licking his face.

"Jack, I'm sor… You have no idea how… There's a good reason. I mean for thinking that you were… I mean, what else was I supposed to think? The Class V, and—"

"Someone was shooting at us on the river. Jenny thinks they might have been stray bullets from a hunter, and I hope she's right. But if she's wrong, I don't know which one of us he was shooting at."

"Tell me why someone might want you dead."

Marie shook her head. "I…" She shrugged.

"So even now, knowing who I am, you can't open up to me."

"I want to. But I can't."

He grabbed her hand and led her to the door of the RV. He took the first step up, then stopped. Turning, he stared down at her. Powerful, intimidating, demanding. "I want the truth from you, or we'll have nothing more to talk about." The finality in his statement made it clear he meant it.

She was sick of the deception, the lies. No more. At least not with Jack. "Okay, the truth," she said.

"Did you used to be a blonde?"

The tension of the day exploded in a laugh of incredulity. "That's what you want to know?"

"For starters."

He smiled and her insides melted.

INSIDE THE RV, Jack set the box that held his whole life down on the kitchen counter. He waited while Marie got Astrid settled on the small couch. Then, like a recalcitrant child, she faced him, standing by the door as if poised for flight.

"I'll have that rifle, if you don't mind." He was generally a trusting sort, but there were limits. She handed it to him without protest. He checked to make sure the safety was on, then reached around her, resisting the urge to fold her into his arms, and laid the Winchester across the driver's seat, out of the way. "Where'd you learn to shoot?"

She hesitated.

"The truth, Marie. I mean it."

"I learned from a guy named George."

"Now there's an earth-shattering revelation." He shook his head, smiling again despite trying to keep a stern expression. "I'm going to have to drag every detail out of you, aren't I?"

She shrugged. "What can I say? A leopard doesn't change its spots."

"Well, there's a cynical viewpoint. But let's get back to my original question. Were you ever a blonde?"

She smiled shyly, and some of the stiffness left her posture. "I was."

Why do I know that?

Jack leaned against the kitchen counter, crossing his arms over his chest to hide his frustration. Much of his memory had returned. He remembered his mom, his sisters, where he grew up, his childhood. He remembered college and the allure of law enforcement. He remembered past cases, and he definitely remembered what happened during the shootout at the Gaines compound.

But there were gaps. For one thing, he had no idea how he got the burn on his arm. He didn't know what a marshal from Seattle was doing in Jasper on the night of the storm that had robbed him of his memories. And most frustrating of all, he didn't know how Marie fit into all of this.

"Did you know Abel Gaines? Not from TV, but in person?"

Marie shivered.

"You're cold. Here, let me get you something." He walked to the master bedroom in the back of the RV, and rummaged through the closet, pulling out a red-and-black flannel shirt.

She'd changed clothes since their river excursion, but the T-shirt Marie had pulled on over jeans was inadequate for the sharp drop in temperature from both the oncoming night and the approaching storm.

She slipped into the shirt with a grateful sigh. "Thanks."

"So, about Abe—"

"My turn. Let me see what's in your box."

He hesitated. Her mysteries were far more enticing than his. Still, he had promised. Pushing away from the counter, he turned to the box and lifted the lid. "Have a look."

Marie went through the contents of his wallet, hefted his badge and peppered him with questions. He identified his mom and sisters in the only picture he kept on him and promised to tell her about them someday. No, he wasn't married, never had been. No fiancée, no girlfriend. No kids. Not even a pet.

"I knew Abel Gaines. In person." She took a step away from Jack and wrapped her arms around her middle. Her head dropped forward, and she refused to meet his eyes. Jack recognized the body language. Shame. "I took care of his horse. And I sort of dated him, for a little while."

Laser-like pain jabbed behind his eyes, and he drew in a sharp breath. Reaching up, Jack massaged his forehead. The connection. She knew Abel. As a blonde. She took care of his horse. She'd *dated* him. He dropped his hand away from his forehead, and looked at Marie, *really* looked at her, seeing her as a blonde. In a photograph. In a case file.

Memories teetered on the edge of remembrance. Why had a field agent from Seattle been in Jasper? Because…he no longer worked in Seattle. He'd been transferred to Boise. Yes, that was right. But why? Because there was an opening. Someone, a deputy named George something or other, had died unexpectedly. A heart attack. Jack was his replacement.

Where'd you learn to shoot?

I learned from a guy named George.

"Marie, are you in WITSEC?"

"Yes," she whispered. "That's why I couldn't tell you anything."

He moved to her and grabbed her shoulders in excitement. "I remember now. George Murphy had a heart attack and passed away. I was assigned as your new case deputy. The night of the storm, I learned of Abel's prison escape. I was coming to Jasper to find you, move you to safety."

Marie's eyes widened. "That's why I couldn't reach him. I've been trying to contact him since the day Astrid and I found you." Her voice turned somber. "I knew he had health problems, but I'd hoped that wasn't why I never heard back from him."

"I'm sorry about George. It must be hard losing

someone you depended on. I know life in Witness Protection isn't easy."

Nodding, Marie took a small step back and out of his grasp. "I told you how I knew Abel, and I'm sure you know the rest from my file." Lowering herself onto the couch, she asked, "Do you know what's been causing your headaches?"

Jack sat next to her. "I was at the Gaines compound for the siege." He quickly added, "As a marshal, involved in the take-down of Abel and his followers." He blew out a breath. "Starting with when I woke up with no memory, every time a vision from that day has tried to rear its ugly head, the headaches come. As well as nightmares of blood, bodies, fire. Everything I saw there."

Marie ran a finger along the scarred tissue on his arm. "Is that where this came from?"

He looked down at the grisly mass of melted flesh, realizing that siege *was* when it had happened. "I tried to save another marshal when a piece of burning wood fell on him."

"Tried?"

"He made it to the hospital. But his injuries were too extensive." Jack looked into Marie's eyes. "He died the next day."

Marie rested her palm against his cheek. "Jack." The word left her lips on a whispered sigh.

That was all the invitation he needed. He crushed his lips to hers and invaded her mouth. She opened to him without hesitation, her arms stretching up and encircling his neck. His arms wrapped around her, pulling her tight to his body. Tighter still. He never wanted to let her go.

He understood her now. Her reticence to know people, to share her life with them, her crippling fear, all of it rooted in being the hunted prey of Abel Gaines. And when Jack turned up in Jasper with no memory right when Abel escaped, it wasn't so farfetched for her to think he might be one of Abel's accomplices.

Adding to the confusion, his transfer to the Boise office happened shortly before his vacation was scheduled to start. As of the day Marie had found him, he was supposed to be on a three-week fly fishing trip, unreachable in the Montana wilderness. But when he caught the alert that Abel had escaped, he'd put the vacation out of his mind and rushed to move Marie to safety. He'd planned on calling in to the office from the road. No one from his office was expecting him back yet. They didn't even know he'd been missing.

Taken with the fact that Marie didn't know why George never answered her pleas for help and didn't know Jack was her new case manager, he'd been lucky she hadn't turned that Winchester on him right from the beginning. How alone, how confused, how afraid she must have been. Yet, despite all that, and even with her mile-high walls, she had let him in. A little, but in.

He broke their kiss, his nostrils flaring, his chest rising and falling rapidly. She was panting, as well. The man he used to be had been unhappy. In his job. In his life. For far too many years. He hadn't realized that he'd been searching for that elusive *something* to restore his zest for living. In Jasper, Idaho, of all places, he found what he'd been missing. Marie was his happiness.

He cradled her cheeks in his palms and gave her his best, most intense Mr. Hypnotic Staring Man look. "Marie, I love you."

Chapter Eighteen

The intoxicating scent of lovemaking filled Jack's nostrils. Warm and sated, Marie lay naked beside him, tucked into the crook of his arm like she belonged there. For all time. Nothing had ever felt so right. Using his free hand, he reached across his chest and brushed a tendril of hair away from her face and tucked it behind her ear.

The only thing that would have made this moment perfect was if she had admitted to loving him, too. But he got it. It was going to take a while for her to get to the same place he was, and he was prepared to wait for as long as that took.

The rain had started, not heavy, but a solid downpour punctuated by the occasional flash of lightning and a rumble of thunder. The effect was insulating, like they were the only two people on the planet. He enjoyed that they could spend time with each other in companionable silence, especially after sex.

Sex. Now, that was a wholly inadequate word for what had passed between them. The first time, after the fire, it had been amazing. Two people who really liked each other, and who answered the strong pull between them. But ultimately, it had been sex.

This time was as different from that as night was from day. This time he'd known who he was, and he'd known why Marie was the way she was. This time there had been openness and vulnerability. He'd willed his soul to her, and it felt like she gave back in kind. This time it had been lovemaking. At least for him.

Marie lifted her lazy gaze to him and smiled. Heaven help him. He could spend the rest of his life looking at that beautiful mouth. "Why the smile?"

"As if you didn't know."

"Maybe, but a man likes to hear his woman tell him, to be sure."

"So, I'm your woman?"

"If you'll have me."

"I think I could be persuaded. I have a lot of reasons to smile, my man." Marie ran her toes up his leg. "And I'm in bed with the best one."

Jack's lips met hers in a quick kiss that took a passionate turn. Then he pulled away with a moan.

"What's the matter?"

"You're going to kill me. I need a little recovery time."

She chuckled. "Women are definitely superior to men in that regard."

"You'll get no argument from me." He pulled his arm out from under her head and rolled to face her. "You're so beautiful."

"Please, I must be a total mess."

He stroked her cheek. "Not to me."

She ran her fingers through the hair on his chest. "Jack?"

"Yes?"

"Don't give up on me. About being in love."

"Only if you promise that you won't push me away."

"Deal."

When he committed, he committed. But that was his fear now, that in his quest to make her love him, he would smother her. Time to change the subject. He looked over at one of the small bedroom windows. "Listen. Do you hear the wind? Sounds like it's really kicking up out there."

"Word on the street is that you're a big, bad lawman. Not afraid of a little weather, are you?"

"No, ma'am. Just offering up a friendly observation." He kissed her again just as the electricity went out. "What is it with this place and storms?"

"The power outages around here usually don't last long." Marie sat up and pulled on her jeans. Groping on the floor, she felt around for the rest of her clothes. "If this one does, Emma has a generator for the house and another for the kennel."

"That's good, because it sounds like the dogs aren't digging the dark." Jack pulled his T-shirt on and stood.

"I'm going to check on them. I don't suppose you have a slicker or maybe a windbreaker I could borrow?"

"Not sure." He dug through the closet. "How about this?"

An old, faded hunting jacket. "Why not? Better than nothing."

She slipped it on, slid her phone into the jacket's pocket and walked toward the door. "You don't have to go. No sense in both of us getting wet."

"Just give me a sec, will you? I need to take a leak."

"It's okay. I'll be back in a couple of minutes." And she was out the door, Astrid on her heels.

"Stubborn woman," he muttered.

While he took care of business, it seemed like the dogs ramped up their howling and barking. He was pushing his feet into his boots when he heard a gunshot blast.

His head swiveled to the driver's seat where the Winchester still lay. His fear when Marie had been swallowed by the river this morning paled to the fear he felt now. Whoever had been shooting at them earlier had found them. And it sure as hell wasn't any wild game hunter.

Jack grabbed the rifle and raced out after her.

WHEN SHE DASHED from the RV, Marie encountered a storm much worse than she'd expected. Rain pelted her like tiny marbles, and the wind ripped at her jacket and turned her hair into whips. Without the outside kennel light to see by, she stumbled blindly through the inky darkness.

Astrid had disappeared, her agitated bark still audible over the roar of the storm. Marie was getting a bad feeling, and her old protective instincts geared up.

Slogging through mud, swinging her arms for balance, she headed for the kennel, telling herself she was acting the fool. Abel was dead and Jack was a good guy.

He might be wrong about someone shooting at them on the river. Maybe Jenny was right, it was just a hunter who should have his license taken away. She still needed to be careful until they were sure, but she was ready to start living her life instead of just existing. *So* ready.

A flash of lightning revealed the kennel, the gate to the outside runs and a man pointing a weapon at her. Darkness reclaimed the sky. Marie screamed. A gun blasted. A burning sensation sliced through her left arm.

She pivoted toward the RV when she heard the pitiful yelp of an animal. She turned back, hightailing it to the kennel, slamming shut the front door the same instant a second bullet punched through.

The kenneled dogs continued their racket as Marie spun to the side, taking shelter against the concrete wall of the building. Touching her arm with care, she winced and brought away fingers coated in blood. She'd been shot.

"I can't believe I left the Winchester in the RV."

She pulled out her phone, dialed 911. The recording informed her there was no service in her area. "Perfect. And no landline, because no power."

She didn't bother to wonder who had shot her. She'd been wrong about Jack working with Abel, but she'd been right that someone was. About to peek out the window, hoping to see Jack coming, the door burst open and slammed shut.

"Marie? Are you all right?" Jack stumbled against her.

"Yes. It's just a flesh wound in my arm. But I left the rifle in the RV."

"I've got it. Grabbed it as soon as I heard the shot." He crouched next to her and helped her take off the jacket. "Give me your phone." Jack examined her arm by the phone's flashlight. "Looks like a through-and-through in the fatty part of your arm."

"Did you seriously just call my arm fat?"

"Just meant no bone or muscle damage." Jack pulled his T-shirt over his head and wrapped it around Marie's arm. "Where's Astrid?"

"She took off. I heard her barking, but then I got shot and just ran for it." She tried to ignore the pain while he tightened the makeshift bandage. "I've got to find her."

"You're not going back out there."

"Jack—"

"We'll call her. Get her to come in here." He moved to the other side of the door, still protected by the kennel's concrete construction.

Marie followed him. While Jack cracked open the door and held it against the wind, she whistled and called Astrid as if her life depended on it. Astrid's, anyway. Having a dog that was trained to protect you was all well and good until the dog was endangered. Pushing the thought from her mind, Marie grabbed the edge of the door and yelled again. Astrid's barking sounded closer.

"Come, Astrid. Come!" Followed by a long whistle. A louder bark. "Here she comes, Jack."

Jack pulled Marie behind him, away from the door, and opened it wider. A very wet, very muddy Astrid dashed through the opening. Jack slammed the door shut and Marie collapsed on the floor, checking Astrid to make sure she hadn't been hurt.

"Thank goodness, girl. I was so worried about you." Marie hugged her, then flinched when Astrid shook rain and mud everywhere.

"Are there any lanterns, anything in here we can use for light?" Jack put his arm around Marie and moved her back under the window, where there was more wall space. Astrid followed.

"Emma might store some flashlights or LED lanterns out here. Let me check." Marie stood just as lightning branched across the sky. She looked out the window, screamed and dropped back to the floor. "It's Abel!"

"They said he died in the fire."

"Well, they were wrong. I just saw him out there, as alive as you and me."

Jack grabbed the rifle and flipped off the safety. "We need to wait for another flash of lightning so I can see him."

They moved back to the side of the door with the handle. Jack knelt on one knee. Waiting, watching for light from Mother Nature when the window they'd just been sitting beneath exploded into the room. Marie locked the door handle while Astrid huddled next to her. The poor dog had been trained to attack threats, not deal with broken glass raining down.

"Stay here." Jack moved to the window and stood next to it.

When lightning struck, he poked the barrel through where the glass had been, paused a moment, then took a shot. Another bullet flew through the kennel as Jack pulled back, then just as quickly, he resumed shooting.

Frustrated, Marie let out a string of curses that had Astrid tipping her head from side to side. "Do you see him?" she asked Jack.

"I did. Can't see anything now. Too dark." Jack glanced at Marie. "Your arm okay?"

"Other than hurting, it's fine."

"Is the back door locked?" He peeked past the window frame, only to duck back as Abel took another shot.

Panicking about the back door, Marie scurried in a crouch to check it. She squat-walked back. "It's locked."

Another shot came through the window, followed by a barrage of bullets through the wooden door, splintering sections of it.

"We've got to set a trap for him. Right now, he's got the advantage." Jack hunkered down. "And we're out of ammo."

Marie reached into her pocket and pulled out the extra cartridges she'd brought. "No we're not." She handed them to Jack.

"I love a woman who's prepared." He reloaded the rifle. "Can you shoot this with your arm hurt?"

"Yes." Whatever it took to bring down Abel Gaines.

"I'm going to grab the shovel and unlock the back door. You stay up here and shoot through the window. If he thinks we're both still up here, firing, maybe he'll go round to the back, where I'll be waiting for him."

"What if he doesn't?" Marie took the Winchester from him.

"I'll figure out a way to lure him back there." Jack slid his hand around the back of her neck and kissed her. "Be careful. You're not shooting to hit him, so don't take any chances."

Marie nodded and Jack went to find the shovel with Marie's phone light. When he called to her that he was in position, she propped the barrel on the window-sill and fired. Abel must have moved, because his returning shot smacked into the window frame. Marie dropped to the floor, her back to the wall, and covered her head while more bullets came through the door.

When they stopped, Marie popped up, fired and dropped back down. Fearing Abel might sneak up and just lean in through the window, she scuttled backward across the floor until she could see him if he came. From her new position, she propped her sore arm on her knee, the rifle on her arm, and sent bullets through the window at irregular intervals, continuing even after the incoming shots paused.

The kenneled dogs still barked at full volume and the rain poured down on the metal roof, making it impossible to talk quietly. Marie ran to where Jack stood. "Be careful. He might be circling around. He's not shooting at the front now."

"I'm ready." Jack stood to the side of the back door, holding the shovel by the handle with the blade in the air. "Get in Emma's office so you're out of the line of fire."

"No way. I'm going to keep watching the front." She returned to her previous position.

Astrid ran between Marie and Jack, ready for whoever needed her help. With everything quiet in the front, Marie crept down the short hall to the corner of Emma's office, where she could peek around at the back door. A low growl started deep in Astrid's chest, breaking into a ferocious snarl as she charged toward Jack. Abel stood on the other side of the back door, framed in the window.

Marie screamed as Astrid jumped through the glass, attaching herself to Abel's left arm. Drops of blood stained the sharp edges of window glass still in the frame. Astrid's blood.

Jack threw open the door, brandishing the shovel. Yelling and turning in circles, Abel tried to get Astrid off him. Unable to hit the man without possibly hurting the dog, Jack backed into the building. Abel followed, swinging the gun in his right hand and hitting Astrid with it. She yelped and fell to the ground.

Marie went into mother-bear mode for her fur baby. Jack swung the shovel toward Abel. The fugitive raised his gun toward Jack. Marie pulled the trigger on the Winchester, hitting Abel in the chest. Falling inside the door, Abel dropped his gun and lay still. Jack grabbed the gun and held it on him while Marie jumped over his body and through the door.

Astrid lay on the ground, covered in cuts from the broken window. A gash on her head from being pistol-whipped oozed blood that mixed with the rain as it ran into the mud. Marie dropped to her knees and cradled

Astrid. She was conscious, whimpering, and when she looked at Marie her eyes were filled with pain.

Jack appeared at Marie's side. "Is she okay?"

"I need to take care of these cuts." Marie stroked Astrid's ear. "Is he…"

"Dead. We don't need to worry about Abel Gaines ever again." Jack bent down and picked up Astrid. Carrying her like a young child, he brought her inside the kennel.

"Take her into the indoor training area. There's a table in there you can put her on." Marie headed toward the supply cabinet in the stall area, where she grabbed clean towels. She ran them over to Jack. "I've got to get my bag from the house. Be right back."

"Marie, no! We don't know if anyone else is out there." That stopped her.

"Tell me where it is, and I'll get it for you. Dammit, trust me, will you?"

She told him its location, as well as that of a gallon bottle of distilled water Emma used for ironing, and he returned with both. With Jack holding her phone for the light, Marie opened her bag and removed bandages and tweezers. "I understand bull riders now. That was the longest eight minutes of my life."

"Princess, a bull ride is eight seconds, not eight minutes."

"To-mato, to-mawto." Her left arm hung limp at her side. Her right rested on Astrid. Jack took the water bottle and set it on the floor.

"Do you need to sedate her?" Jack asked.

"I'm going to try to do it without. See how she does."

Marie removed the cap from the water jug. "Can you pour some of it over the head gash and the cuts on this side?"

Jack did as she asked while Marie kept a hand on Astrid, calming her.

"The gash is the only one still bleeding. If you hold a towel against it with some pressure, I'll check these other cuts for glass." Marie put on a pair of magnifying glasses and tweezed tiny pieces of glass out of the many cuts.

The lights blinked on in the room, and Marie realized the rain on the roof had tapered off. When she was sure she'd gotten all the sharp fragments, she disinfected the cuts. Most were narrow enough that they would heal on their own. She repeated the process on Astrid's other side, then cleaned and bandaged cuts on her legs.

The head wound's bleeding had slowed, and it wasn't as deep as it had seemed. They rinsed it again, then Jack continued to hold a clean towel against it while Marie packed up her bag. Standing on opposite sides of the dog, Marie met Jack's intense gaze.

"Thanks for helping with Astrid. With my arm, I'd never have been able to do it alone."

Jack lifted the towel to find the wound no longer bleeding. He walked around the table and wrapped his arms around Marie. "Thank you for saving my life." He bent down and kissed her.

"I think we were all kind of saving each other, so…"

Shaking his head, Jack pulled her into a tighter hug.

"Uh-uh. That's the second time you've rescued me, and this time you risked your own life to do it."

She smiled up at him. "Well, considering I practically tried to kill you twice, trying to hit you with the kayak paddle and shooting at you earlier, I think we're sort of even."

With her head pressed against his warm skin, his heart beating beneath her ear, Marie couldn't deny her feelings. She'd been wary, careful, hesitant, determined to not get attached. But the attachment happened despite every effort to stop it. She mumbled against Jack's chest.

"What did you say?" Grasping her shoulders, Jack held her a few inches away from him so he could see her face.

Marie lowered her eyes. *This is stupid.* She'd faced off with the bane of her existence and won, but voicing her own emotions out loud scared her. *Stupid. Stupid. Stupid.* She lifted her head and looked Jack straight in the eye.

"I love you," she repeated. There. She'd said it. Out loud. To Jack.

"Was that so hard?"

"Yes." She wrapped her right arm around him and hugged as tightly as she could.

"Then it means even more." Jack rested his chin against her head.

Astrid whimpered and Marie let go of Jack to check on her.

Jack checked Marie's cell for service. "Looks like the towers are still out."

"The landline should work now that the power's back on. Check in Emma's or Barbara's office." Marie continued to comfort Astrid while Jack called the police. When he returned, she said, "The wedding party is going to be upset when they learn we have a better story to tell about this weekend."

With one arm around Marie and the other hand stroking Astrid's snout, Jack smiled. "Yep. And the ending makes it all worth it."

Chapter Nineteen

"I love this awning." Marie sipped her wine.

After the pandemonium of Saturday, Sunday afternoon drew down in serene comfort. The sun was low in an orange-hued sky. A slight breeze stirred a carpet of green-and-brown grass, while chirping bluebirds added to the ambience. She and Jack sat in lawn chairs outside the RV, enjoying nature's display, a large, motorized awning open above their heads.

"Blocks the sun, and if it drizzles again, we won't get wet," she said. "How'd you figure out how to work it?" She set her glass down on the small table brought out from the kennel.

"Shane showed me last week when he stopped by, but this is the first time I've had a chance to use it." Jack reached over and threaded his fingers through Marie's uninjured right hand. "Much nicer with company." A playful smile kicked up at the corners of his mouth.

"I'm finding quite a few things are nicer with company." Marie chuckled as she stretched her bandaged left arm and moved it around to ease the stiffness.

After Abel had been killed and once power was restored, they'd called in the cavalry, and pretty much every police and emergency vehicle in Jasper arrived, lights flashing and sirens blaring.

Eddie, the paramedic who'd helped Marie the morning she'd found Jack beside the road, wanted to take her to the hospital. She'd refused. Astrid had been hurt trying to save them; no way would Marie leave her side. No way would she leave Jack's side. The gunshot wound hurt like hell, but even she could see it wasn't serious.

With reservations, Eddie had sterilized and bandaged Marie's wound at the scene. "All right, Doc. I get it. I remember how I was when Killer was hurt, but promise me that first thing Monday, you'll see a doctor."

Now, lying on a pallet between the lawn chairs, a recovering Astrid kept watch on the drive. Emma, Piper and Shane would be home soon from the wedding, and Astrid seemed to know that. Marie reached down and gave her ear a tug. "Ready for things to get back to normal, eh, girl?"

Astrid's tail thumped the ground in response.

"Me, too." Although Marie was still trying to wrap her head around the fact that her normal was about to be redefined in a profound way.

She faced Jack, struck, as always, by the intensity of his intriguing eyes. When bound by secrecy, she'd feared his ability to deep-dive into her soul. Now that she was free, she hoped she'd be able to overcome her ingrained reticence. Buried inside her was a need to share her life. With Jack. And to share his in return.

"I still can't believe you're my case deputy." Not

necessarily a good thing. No fraternization allowed. A situation guaranteed to put the kibosh on a relationship between the two of them. "But not for much longer." She gave his fingers a quick squeeze.

Jack's eyebrows rose. "You're definitely leaving the program?"

"Abso-freaking-lutely. I decided that as soon as I heard Abel—who wasn't Abel—died in the Hills fire."

Jack shook his head. "I won't lie—I thought you were seeing things last night when you said he was the one shooting at us."

"I don't blame you. Thank goodness the FBI identified Abel's brother as the burned body, or I'd think I was deluded myself. I guess those DNA tests aren't always 100 percent perfect" Marie picked up her wine glass. "I'm glad the Jasper police found those shell casings up on the cliff and matched them to Abel's rifle. It'll be nice not looking over my shoulder all the time."

The FBI had also informed them, via Jasper PD, that all key players with Abel at the compound that day five years ago were either in prison or had cut ties with him. "You gonna stick with the name Marie or go back to using Megan?" Jack stroked Astrid's ear, still the best place to pet her amidst all the cuts and bandages.

Picking up her glass, she ran a finger around its rim. "Haven't decided. But to be honest, every time I so much as think the word *Megan*, I hear it in *his* voice. Besides, everyone here knows me as Marie."

And I like hearing you say Marie when we make love.

"Sounds to me like you've already decided."

She rewarded him with a sardonic grin. "I'm not sure I like someone knowing me so well."

Jack chuckled. "I'll have to notify the office. Since all your IDs and papers are in the name of Marie Beaumont, they may have some suggestions on which name to use going forward."

"I hope whatever they have to do to cut me loose doesn't take long, since case deputies can't fraternize with their witnesses." Marie waggled her brows.

Jack slapped a palm to his temple. "I'm such an idiot." He dropped his hand and looked at Marie. "The night of the fire, when we made love, I had this strange feeling we were doing something wrong. Subconsciously, I must have known it wasn't allowed."

"Well, I'm glad you managed to ignore the feeling." Marie sighed. "But I guess now we'll have to behave until I'm officially out of WITSEC."

"Um, about that."

Marie's heart curled into the fetal position.

"I made a decision, too."

He's going to tell me we're over.

"I'm going to resign from the Marshals Service."

Exhaling in relief, Marie realized what that meant for him. "You can't quit the job you love just so we can have sex. It won't take that long to—"

Jack laughed. "I'm not quitting for sex. I haven't been happy in my job for quite a while. I remember that now." He rubbed his palms on his knees. "Since the Gaines compound thing, in fact. It's funny—I never made the connection between what happened there and PTSD until you mentioned it. I don't think I have actual PTSD, because the only times I had symptoms were during the amnesia. But I doubt I'll ever enjoy the job again." He took Marie's hand. "And then, of course, there's the sex."

Marie gave him a playful swat. "I won't lie and say I'm disappointed about that, but what will you do? Find something else in Boise?" It would be okay. Boise was only three hours away. Maybe she'd even move there.

"Oh, no, I'm not staying in Boise." He leaned closer to her. "See, there's this beautiful vet who lives in a teeny, tiny town called Jasper. And I intend to woo her until she agrees to spend the rest of her life with me." He turned Marie's hand over and kissed the palm. "Since I'll be living here, I think I'll take Jason's suggestion and apply with the Jasper Police Department."

Marie felt her throat tighten. "You'd do that for me?"

"I'd be doing it for both of us. I really like Jasper and the people here. One in particular." Astrid raised her head and whined. "I like you, too, Astrid."

A small cloud of dust rising in the distance brought the three of them to their feet.

"Ah, the return of the wedding party," Marie said. "I bet Tashya made a beautiful bride. And Jason in a tux? I wish I could have seen them."

Jack chuckled. "And miss all the excitement around here this weekend?"

"Well, it wasn't *all* horrible." She squeezed Jack's hand, which was still holding hers. "And at least the parts that *were* horrible are over now."

They watched until Emma's car pulled across the

drive and stopped near the RV. Emma, Piper and Shane climbed out, all smiles.

"Oh, Marie, you missed the best wedding," Piper said. "Everything went off without a hitch."

"Except the bride and groom, I hope." Jack's grin faded as three sets of eyes turned toward him. "Without a hitch? The bride and groom…got hitched?"

Emma groaned at the bad joke. "I hope your sense of humor returns with your memory."

Marie exchanged a small smile with Jack, then said, "Tell us all about the wedding."

Emma and Piper shared the important highlights, even teasing poor Shane about when he and Piper would be walking down the aisle.

"So the reception was magical and very romantic," Marie said in recap.

"Oh, yes. Great food, lots of champagne and tons of dancing." Piper turned to Emma. "Go on, tell her. Tell her about the dancing."

Emma wore a big cat-ate-the-canary smile. "Turns out Chief Walters can really cut a rug on the dance floor."

"The best part is *who* he was dancing with." Piper looked at Marie as if expecting her to guess. When she didn't, Piper blurted out, "Teresa Norwood."

Marie knew the name. "The police department's secretary?"

Emma nodded. "That's the one. She's been flirting with him for years, but the man was oblivious. Well, this weekend he finally noticed. They danced nearly every dance together."

Piper added, "It was so cute. And then this morning, Shane ran into…you tell them, Shane."

Shane crossed his arms over his chest. "I refuse to stand here and gossip."

"Fine. I'll finish telling it." Piper rolled her eyes. "This morning Shane got up early to work out in the resort's exercise room. He was walking down the hall toward the elevator, and here comes Chief Walters, sneaking out of Teresa's room."

"I didn't say he was sneaking," Shane said.

"Whatever. He was leaving Teresa's room at, like, five o'clock in the morning." Piper's enthusiastic smile grew even larger. "But there's more," she told Marie. "Guess who caught the bouquet?"

"Teresa?" Marie guessed.

"Chief Walters?" Jack tried.

"No and no." Piper moved into the stance of a game show beauty displaying the grand prize, and her hands went to Emma. "Ta-da!"

"Really? You caught the bouquet?" Marie's grin turned mischievous. "Now we just need to find *you* a man, Emma."

Emma's cheeks turned red. "I really don't want to discuss this."

"You know, it wouldn't kill you to have a social life." Marie enjoyed tossing Emma's words of advice back at her.

"All right, enough about the wedding. Sorry you two got stuck here," Emma said to Jack and Marie. "How did everything go?"

"Well, we got shot at while we were kayaking," Jack said.

Shane, Piper and Emma looked at him, their mouths open in a row of perfect Os.

"Then I almost drowned on a Class V rapids," Marie added.

They turned their Os toward Marie.

"We had another really bad storm." This from Jack.

"But before that, a hiker found Jack's truck and his stuff. His memory is back. Turns out he's a deputy US marshal."

The other three finally closed their mouths, but they still followed the conversation like a ping-pong match.

"Marie's been in witness protection for the last five years."

"And Jack's actually my case deputy."

Still not a peep from the three wedding guests.

"Abel Gaines didn't die in the fire at the Hills, and he ambushed us here last night," Jack said. "Busted out two of the kennel windows and shot the front door up. Sorry."

"Abel shot me in the arm, pistol-whipped Astrid and almost shot Jack."

"But Marie killed Abel and saved my life."

Emma stared at Piper, who stared at Shane, who stared at Marie and Jack.

"Now she's leaving WITSEC." Jack put his arm around Marie's shoulders, and she nestled closer to him.

"And he's leaving the Marshals Service." Looking up at Jack, she smiled. "And moving here."

"Yeah, I might apply for the opening at the Jasper PD."

Marie shrugged. "You know. Just another boring, run-of-the-mill weekend in Jasper, Idaho."

* * * * *

Look for the next book in the K-9s on Patrol series,
Police Dog Procedural *by Lena Diaz,*
coming soon.

And in case you missed the
previous titles in the series:

Available now wherever
Harlequin Intrigue books are sold!

Don't miss the next book in

B.J. DANIELS

Buckhorn, Montana series

Order your copy today!

HARLEQUIN

Heartfelt or thrilling, passionate or uplifting—Harlequin is more than just happily-ever-after.

With twelve different series to choose from and new books available every month, you are sure to find stories that will move you, uplift you, inspire and delight you.

SIGN UP FOR THE HARLEQUIN NEWSLETTER

Be the first to hear about great new reads and exciting offers!

Harlequin.com/newsletters